CHICKEN BOY
FRANCES O'ROARK DOWELL

Atheneum Books for Young Readers
New York London Toronto Sydney

ACKNOWLEDGMENTS

The author would like to thank the following people for their help
and encouragement: Susan Burke, Caitlyn Dlouhy, Clifton Dowell,
Amy Graham, Danielle Hudson, and Jane and Del O'Roark,
her most honorable parents.

Atheneum Books for Young Readers
An imprint of Simon & Schuster Children's Publishing Division
1230 Avenue of the Americas
New York, New York 10020

Book design by Kristin Smith
The text for this book is set in Slimbach.
Manufactured in the United States of America
First Edition
2 4 6 8 10 9 7 5 3 1
Library of Congress Cataloging-in-Publication Data
Dowell, Frances O'Roark.
Chicken boy / Frances O'Roark Dowell.—1st ed.
p.   cm.
Summary: Since the death of his mother, Tobin's family and school life has been in
disarray, but after he starts raising chickens with his seventh-grade classmate,
Henry, everything starts to fall into place.
ISBN 0-689-85816-7
[1. Self-esteem—Fiction. 2. Family problems—Fiction. 3. Grandmothers—Fiction.
4. Friendship—Fiction. 5. Chickens—Fiction. 6. Schools—Fiction.] I. Title.
PZ7.D75455Ch 2005
[Fic]—dc22   2004010928

For Jack and Will

ONE

You might have heard about the time my granny got arrested on the first day of school. Maybe you were one of them pie-eyed kids she almost ran down with her 1984 sky blue Toyota truck, me riding shotgun. When Granny pulled up on the sidewalk like it was our own personal parking spot, everybody was yelling for them kids to get out of the way, but nobody could hear a thing over the blast of Granny's radio and her singing at the top of her lungs.

I sat in the police car while an officer made Granny walk a straight line with her finger on her nose, like maybe she'd been driving drunk, which she hadn't been. I wanted like anything to switch on the flashing lights, but the cop in the driver's seat seemed to guess what I had on my mind. "What's your name, son?" he asked, letting me know he was paying attention.

I looked at my reflection in his mirrored sunglasses. "Tobin McCauley."

The cop grinned and jerked his thumb toward Granny. "Is she a McCauley, too? Because that would explain everything right off the bat."

"She's the mother-in-law to a McCauley," I told him, my fingers still itching to hit that flashing-lights button.

"Close enough," is what the cop replied. I guess he meant anyone in spitting distance of being related to one of my brothers—or my sister, for that matter—had a good chance of having a criminal heart. Not that they ever got busted for anything too bad, mostly petty stuff like shoplifting and being a public nuisance. And Shane and Summer were so old now that they hardly ever did anything worse than jaywalk. It'd been years since Summer had lifted a lipstick from Eckerd drugstore, or Shane had gone hot-rodding the wrong way down Six Forks Road.

The cop eyed me suspiciously, remembering that I was a McCauley, too. "You get in much trouble?"

I tried to look tough. I'd stolen a few paper clips in my time, a pencil or two, been made to stay after school for cheating on a test. Most of the stuff I did, I did it because teachers seemed to expect it from me. If I didn't commit at least a few minor crimes, then they'd go on about how good I was, what a nice change from the other McCauleys they'd taught in years past. I hated school bad enough without the teachers making a fuss over me.

"Yeah, I get in trouble," I told the cop, puffing out my chest. "They had to put a special guard on me last year."

The cop gave me the quick once-over. "Bet there's not a prison built that could hold you, son," he said, then started choking on his own laughter, his face glowing red as a bowl of tomato soup.

Outside, Granny was making her case to the other officer. "I'm all this boy's got, 'cause his daddy's good for nothing," I heard her say.

"His mama passed on when he was seven. Somebody's got to take care of him."

"Yes, ma'am," the police officer agreed politely. "But that doesn't mean you don't have to follow proper parking procedures."

Granny shoved a piece of Juicy Fruit in her mouth. "You like that Alan Jackson? KISS Country Radio don't play nothing but that Alan Jackson, it seems like. I think he's right good-looking, but you can't see him on the radio, now can you?"

"That's right, ma'am," the officer said. He turned toward the squad car and rolled his eyes.

After I got booted out of the patrol car, I watched from the flagpole as they drove Granny away. I was sorry they left off the siren and the lights. I knew that inside that car Granny was sorry, too.

Just the day before, my brother Patrick had tried to talk me out of riding to school with Granny. He'd found me on the carport, throwing clumps of dirt at the chain-link fence that separated our yard from the gas station next door. The owner's cat was staring at me from out

4

beside the free air pump, but I ignored it. I don't like cats as a rule.

"Tomorrow's your first day of seventh grade," Patrick said, pulling up an overturned paint bucket and taking a seat. I nodded. It was a dumb thing for him to say. I could have said something dumb back, like, "Yeah, and tomorrow's your first day of ninth grade, big whoop," but I wasn't in the mood.

Patrick scooped up a handful of crumbled concrete and aimed it at the cat, which was now sniffing at the fence like it was thinking about coming over for a visit. "If I was you, I'd take the bus to school," he said. "Granny's been driving you since you were in second grade. You've got to figure that's long enough."

"Don't want to take the bus," I told him. "I tried it once, but the exhaust fumes turned me green."

Patrick shook his head. "Beats everybody seeing Granny drop you off at the front of the school. Seventh grade's different from sixth grade. People start to notice it when your crazy grandmother drives you around all over town.

You want them to think you're weird, too?"

I picked at a piece of rubber coming off of my tennis shoe. People already thought I was weird. Between Granny and my juvenile delinquent brothers and sister and the fact that I lived in an old brick shoe box on a two-lane highway instead of in some shiny new suburban home, I didn't have much hope of them thinking otherwise. "I don't care what them fart blowers think," I told Patrick. "Why's it matter so much to you?"

Patrick stood up and shoved his hands in his pockets. Just then the gas station cat wormed its way through a hole in the fence and made a beeline for the carport. Patrick kicked at it and missed. "I don't care if people like you or not."

"So why are you here talking to me?"

He didn't say anything for a minute, just looked left, then right, like he was in a spy movie and the enemy was nearby. Finally he cleared his throat and said, "Daddy said he'd buy me a Big Mac and Super Size fries if I told you not to take rides from Granny anymore."

I snorted. "Daddy don't care who gives me a

ride to school. He's just looking to make Granny mad."

Patrick grinned. "Man, them two will give each other hell till one of them keels over dead."

My dad and Granny had been feuding for as long as I could remember. The only thing they ever had in common was my mom, and once she was gone, they didn't even have that. My sister, Summer, said they were both so mad about my mom dying they'd spend the rest of their lives taking it out on each other.

The gas station cat snaked its way around my ankles like it thought now maybe we could be friends. I scratched its ears without really meaning to. I didn't want to be friends with that cat or anybody else I could think of. Didn't want to go to school the next day either, especially since it was still August and way too hot for thinking.

Mostly I just wanted to ride around in Granny's truck and think about going camping out in the woods. I'd been camping two times in my life, and those trips were stuck on rerun in my brain. Whenever my mind needed somewhere to go, I pushed the camping-trip button on the inside of my head, and all the sudden I was putting river rocks in a circle to make a campfire. Made my whole body get peaceful remembering it.

After I'd watched the police car head out to the main road, I made my way down the hall to my first-period English class, going as slow as I could. I knew it would be a letdown after Granny's arrest, and I was right about that, son. Soon as I pushed open the door, a whole room of snot-nosed kids started giggling and twittering like flea-bitten parrots. Somebody called out, "Nice parking job!"

I ignored their sorry butts. The teacher motioned me over to a desk front and center and then checked her clipboard.

"Are you Tobin?" she asked. "Tobin McCauley?"

She pronounced it wrong, though, more like McCully. "That ain't how you say it," I told her, taking my seat. "It's McCauley that rhymes with holly."

"Ain't!" a low voice croaked like a bullfrog

from the back of the room, and then there was a chorus of bullfrogs calling "ain't, ain't, ain't," with a smart-aleck cricket chirping "redneck, redneck" behind it. A whole different voice, a boy's, only it was pitched high and singsongy, called out, "*Ain't* ain't a word!"

The teacher ignored the frogs and the cricket, but the last comment got her attention. "What makes you think it's not a word?" she asked. She walked to her desk, picked up a dictionary, and headed to the back row, where she handed it to a jughead named Cody Peters. "Look it up and tell me if it's in there."

Cody took the book from her. He didn't look too happy about having his little joke turned into an assignment. "I'll do what I can, ma'am," he said, this time in a slow, countrified voice. "*Ain't* starts with *a*, right?"

That got a good laugh from the spitwads around the room. "Stop talking and start looking," the teacher told him. She leaned against the desk in front of him, her arms folded across her chest. Cody ruffled through a few pages, then ran his finger down a row of words. After a few seconds he looked up at the teacher, his face all full of mock wonder. "Gosh, gee, ma'am, it sure enough is right here."

The teacher took the book from him and snapped it shut. "So maybe *ain't* is a word after all," she said, sounding victorious. She turned as she passed by me and gave me a big wink, like the victory was mine, too.

I put my head on my desk. That's all I needed, a teacher who wanted to be my hero. I closed my eyes and pictured a river. I was walking across it in knee-high rubber boots, carrying a mess of fish in a net. I could see a tent on the other side, smoke rising from the campfire.

I fell asleep before I made it over. Next thing I knew, there was a crow cawing in my ear, only it turned out to be the bell ringing for second period. I stood up slow, yawning my way back into the seventh grade and out to the hallway, where the rest of my useless day was waiting for me.

TWO

Here's how the fight happened.

It was the second week of school. I was sitting on the bleachers in my usual spot for PE, still in my jeans and a T-shirt because I didn't dress out for gym. I tried it for the first few days of school, but I got tired of all the compliments that got passed my way. My legs, which Patrick was always saying were skinnier than air, seemed to make an especially big impression.

At the beginning, Coach Kelly'd gotten all red in the face about me not dressing out. He made remarks about One Bad Apple and snot-nosed punks. He said he remembered my brother Patrick, and he'd been a waste of breathing space, too. But when he saw I wasn't pulling on that Legion Middle School gym shirt for nothing, he let it go. Acted like I wasn't even there. Which was fine by me, son.

I was drawing a race car on the side of my shoe when Cody Peters's voice boomed across the gym, knocking me out of my afternoon daze. "That nice English teacher Miss Thesman sure has taken a shine to Tobin McCully. They sure are spending a lot of time together."

I looked down at my jeans. There was a good hole in the left knee, quarter size. I tugged at a loose thread to make it bigger. I didn't bother answering Peters. Going to Miss Thesman's classroom during morning break hadn't been my idea, but when I wouldn't work on my autobiography in class, she'd said I had to.

"You've got to do the assignment, Tobin, and brainstorming and peer editing are part of the assignment," she'd said. "You want to pass English, right?"

I shrugged. Not if it meant sitting in a group of bean snorters and spilling my guts out. I was keeping my personal information to myself, son.

"It's simple, really," she said, smiling. "Writing an autobiography just means telling your own story in your own words."

"I don't got a story," I told her, and her eyes glistened a little.

"Oh, Tobin," Miss Thesman chirped. "Everybody has a story!"

She decided that if I wouldn't tell mine in class, then I'd come to her room at break time and spill my guts in private. Most teachers, I'd have just skipped on. But the fact was, Miss Thesman smelled nice. She smelled like lemons, my favorite smell in the world next to honeysuckle and the wood of a cedar tree. And she was pretty, too. Not to mention that I didn't want to flunk seventh-grade English. I might not have liked school, but I planned on getting through it on time.

Mostly Miss Thesman just made me write lists, stuff like my favorite TV shows when I was five and what movies I liked to rent from the video store. It wasn't so bad writing down things just for her. I didn't feel like I was giving her ammunition, the way I would have with most other people.

13

When you were alone with her, Miss Thesman wasn't so corny. She chewed gum and bit her fingernails. Sometimes she'd ask me questions out of the blue. One rainy day she stared out the window for a long time, sighing now and again. After a little while, she turned and looked at me. "Do you ever get lonely, Tobin? I mean, really lonely?"

I thought about it for a minute. "I guess so," I said finally, thinking that on rainy days like these, when I was stuck inside and couldn't ride my bike to Granny's or go exploring in the woods, that's when I'd get the loneliest of all.

"Me, too." Miss Thesman waved her hand toward the hallway, where kids were opening and shutting lockers and talking with their friends. "With all these people around, you think you wouldn't, but you do."

Now Cody walked a few feet closer to where I was sitting. His high-price shoes squeaked on the wood floor. "Did you know that lately I've seen Miss Thesman sneaking around the halls with Mr. Ferguson? Doesn't that just break your heart, Tobin McCully? You're not her only man."

"Sneaking around to do what?" This was from Cody's raggedy sidekick, Russell Turner, whose job was asking questions Cody wanted to answer.

This time Cody answered him with a gesture. I won't even go into what he did, but it wasn't right. You don't stand up in the middle of the gym in front of everybody and make your hands go this way and that so people will get a bad idea about someone like Miss Thesman. I looked down at the hole in my jeans, hoping that when I looked up again, Cody would be done with his little routine.

He wasn't.

So I jumped him.

Maybe when you grow up getting pounded on by two older brothers, you figure you're tough enough to take on someone like Cody Peters. Let me tell you, son, you're in for one butt-whuppin' surprise. I don't remember exactly what I was thinking when I jumped Cody. Could be I thought I was Superman, or maybe I thought it was a good day to die. I slammed into him hard enough to knock him down, at least. I was on top of him in a second, hitting at him with everything I had in me.

"Get off me, McCauley!" Cody yelled, and then he was up and flipped me over on my back. I put my hands over my face, but I kicked like a mule, since that was always my best defense against my brothers. Sometimes you can hit a sensitive area, buy yourself time to run. But the harder I kicked, the madder Cody seemed to get. His fists pounded against me like major-league pitches into a catcher's glove. I curled up into a ball, wondering if Coach Kelly would even bother dragging my dead body out of the gym.

All the sudden Cody stumbled backward and fell to the floor. Then there were arms around him, pulling, then knocking him over so his face was on the ground. I could've up and run, but it made me mad that someone was trying to take over my fight, even if I was losing it. I sprang up and jumped on Cody's back. I even hung on for a few seconds before he heaved me off.

The other kid, the one with the hands pulling and pushing, barreled into Cody again, landing two good punches to the gut. Cody made a funny noise, only it wasn't really a noise because no sound came out, just air.

All around us people were yelling and screaming, and then Coach Kelly's voice tore through the gym. "What's going on? Who started this? McCauley, what's your problem?"

Three minutes later we were waiting outside the principal's office—me, Cody Peters, and this kid I didn't know. I'd seen him in a few of my classes, and I'd heard him say he was new, but I couldn't have told you his name. His T-shirt read, I'M TIGER WOODS, but I knew that wasn't right.

THREE

Cody Peters got two days in before-school detention. Tiger Woods got four. I got suspended for
a week, which was fine by me. I was feeling sort
of light and good about everything as I walked
out of the principal's office. A week off of school
and nobody calling to the house to complain
that I never showed up. Hard to beat, son.

I was almost smiling by the time I saw Tiger
Woods out in the hallway. He didn't look like a
kid who could take Cody Peters in a fight. You
wouldn't call him fat exactly, but he was pretty
close to the line. He'd changed out of his gym
clothes, but his street clothes didn't bowl you
over with style. It was the baggy look, I guess

you'd call it; a baggy short-sleeved shirt over a baggy T-shirt and baggy green shorts. Black Chucks and baggy white socks on his feet.

He'd been leaning against the wall, almost sitting on the floor, his knees sticking out, but he stood up when he saw me. "What'd you get?" he asked. "Detention?"

"Nope," I told him, and kept walking. Tiger joined step with me and said, "Well, she must have given you something. I mean, no offense, man, but you started it."

"Ain't nothing to worry about," I told him, wishing he'd get out of my business. It's hard to feel light and good about something when a guy's trying to get all serious on your butt.

Tiger clapped me on the shoulder, not to be mean, more like he'd just been struck by some big idea. "You didn't get expelled, did you?" When I shook my head no again, he asked, "Suspended?"

"Sucks, don't it," I said, hoping he'd get the message I didn't want to talk about it anymore.

"They can't do that!" Tiger looked at me full in the face. "Why didn't you tell the principal what Peters said? I bet she would have understood."

Well, the problem wasn't what Cody said, it was what he did, and no way I was going to stand up in the principal's office and do the same.

Besides, it was over and I was free for a whole week. I kept on walking.

Tiger stuck out his hand. "My name is Henry Otis, by the way. I thought it was cool what you did, sticking up for Miss Thesman. That's why I jumped into it. Well, that and you were getting the snot beaten out of you." He grinned, then looked down at his hand, which was just hanging there in the air. He shoved it into his pocket.

"I could get your homework assignments for you, if you wanted," he went on. I was headed for the big EXIT sign over the school's front doors. If Henry followed me out before the last bell, he'd get suspended too. He either didn't know it or didn't care. "Or if you get bored, you could come over to my house after school. I live on a farm. It's over on Strickland Road, near the Char-Grill? It used to be a horse farm, but they sold most of it to developers. We've got a couple acres. You could come see the chickens I'm raising."

The door swung open like it'd been oiled just

for my exit. Outside the air was filling up with the exhaust fumes from the hundred-some minivans and SUVs come to pick their babies up from jail.

"I think you're the only person in this school who doesn't suck, McCauley," Henry called after me. "Nobody else would've stood up for Miss Thesman, that's for sure."

I turned around in the doorway. Henry made it sound like I was some kind of hero. To the best of my knowledge, nobody had ever thought I was heroic before, and I sort of liked the feel of it. I stared at Henry hard for a second before opening my mouth. "My granny has chickens," I said finally. "I seen her twist one's head off once."

"Pretty gross," Henry said, but he didn't seem all that upset by it.

"Yeah, I guess." I shrugged. "It ran around the yard a minute without its head, just like they say."

"You want to come over and see ours? We won't kill them or anything."

"Nah." I pushed my way out the door. "I got stuff to do."

I didn't have a thing in the world to do, but no need to report that fact to Henry Otis.

FOUR

Monday morning my dad woke me up at first light, which was when he left for work. "Don't you go anywhere today, you hear me, son? Not out in the yard, not to your granny's, no place but right in this house. This is punishment time, not playtime."

I mumbled, "Okay," and rolled over. Next thing I knew, my sister, Summer, was in to wake up Patrick for school. Patrick groaned, but he got up because Summer'd do some damage to you if she had to yell at you more than once to get your behind out of bed. I heard Patrick's feet thud as they hit the ground. He took the trouble to pelt me with a ballpoint pen-cap on his way out of the room, but that didn't keep me from falling back to sleep.

When I finally woke up, the sun was pretty far up there. At first I got that nervous feeling of having messed up bad by being late for school, but then I remembered about being suspended. I stretched out on my bed, feeling the luxury of seven days ahead of me and no school in sight. I planned out what I'd do first, middle, and last. Flip on the TV to watch cartoons, then get me some breakfast, and after that more TV.

Flopping down on the saggy blue couch in front of the television, I felt like I was on the middle of a cruise ship. Usually we were all crammed on there watching something and eating whatever meal it was the time of day for. Me; Patrick; and Daddy; Shane if he was having a fight with Becca, his girlfriend; and Summer when she wasn't working, which she usually was. Elbows stuck in your side and knees jammed against your knees and drinks spilled over onto the cushions. You might get five seconds in a row of enjoying your food.

But on this particular morning I set myself up good, head on the pillow at one end, feet on the pillow at the other, Jimmy Neutron racing across the TV screen. Then I got hungry, so I rolled right off the couch and onto the floor and went on ahead and rolled straight into the kitchen. I decided to roll everywhere I went all week, since there wasn't anybody home to make a smart-aleck remark about it.

Here's the thing. Every once in awhile, during the commercials or when I was rolling my way to the kitchen, I got to thinking about the fight with Cody Peters, and I felt this buzzing feeling that started in my stomach, zigzagged up my spine, and ran all the way to the top of my head, so that I had to shake out my whole body to settle back down.

By Wednesday, that feeling was so alive in me I couldn't make it go away by watching cartoons or nothing. When I thought about the fight, I didn't feel like me anymore. I was this other guy, one who wasn't afraid to jump on the strongest kid in the seventh grade. A guy who did something instead of just sitting there.

I got to feeling so strange that I finally got dressed. I decided to make myself some breakfast, something besides Fruit Roll-Ups and Doritos, but by Wednesday the kitchen was too big of a mess to get an appetite going. The dishes in the sink looked like they'd been pushed in by accident, and the sink had this line of crusty gunk running around it where the dishwashing water had stood for a while before it drained out. A pot of dried-out macaroni and cheese sat on the stove, next to a pot of alphabet soup that'd been there so long, little stars of mold were sprouting in between the letters. Nothing in the refrigerator except two cans of beer, a jar of clam juice, and seven bottles of Summer's nail polish.

I ended up eating half a bag of miniature marshmallows for breakfast. You want to feel low-down and sorry, that's how you do it, son. Eat a cruddy breakfast in the middle of your cruddy kitchen that nobody's bothered to clean in weeks. It didn't make me want to go back to school, but I had to get out of the house so I could get that buzzing feeling back and figure out what it meant.

I could have ridden my bike over to Granny's with my eyes closed. Left on Honeycutt Road, go a quarter mile, swerve around the big pothole city services never got around to fixing, another hundred yards, then right on Durant, right on Mason Farm Road, go past three mailboxes and one oak tree struck by lightning the summer I turned eight, and left into Granny's driveway. When I pulled up to the carport, there she was under her truck, only her feet sticking out.

"You can't drive that thing," I said to the bottom of her tennis shoes, "so why are you working on it?"

Granny's voice slid out from underneath the Toyota. "Judge can revoke my license for thirty days, but he can't revoke my toolbox. I've neglected old Bessie here for way too long. Making up for lost time now."

I leaned my bike up against the side of Granny's house. Calvin, the biggest mutt in Granny's dog posse, ran up and started sniffing on me, but I swatted him away. "You're lucky that's all the judge did to you," I said. To be honest, I was disappointed Granny didn't get any time for pulling up on the front sidewalk of Legion Middle School. I'd been looking forward to visiting her in jail. I'd planned to sneak her a pack of Fig Newtons, which she was pretty much addicted to.

"Hand me the drill-bit extension," Granny called to me. I found her toolbox on the truck's tailgate, but when I searched around inside it, I couldn't find what she wanted.

Granny shimmied out from under the truck and into daylight. Still lying flat on the concrete, she rubbed her chin like she was trying to remember where she'd put it, smudging her face up with oil in the process. "I bet Eddie has it," she said finally, wiping her hands on her shirt. "That's too bad, because I don't think I'll be seeing much of him anymore."

"You have a fight?" I asked her. Eddie was Granny's latest boyfriend. She always had one hanging around somewhere, in case she needed somebody to go fishing with. The thing you noticed most about Eddie was that he was old as the hills but still had a head of flaming red hair. Other than that, he didn't much stand out from all the other boyfriends Granny'd had over the years.

Granny pushed herself up on her elbows. "He says he's done with me, now that I've been arrested. Says he's tired of my stunts, as he calls them. I told him that wasn't no stunt. I was just running late."

I started sorting through Granny's toolbox, lining up the screwdrivers, putting the nippers and snips back in order. I sniffed a pocket wrench, taking in that oily, metallic smell.

"Not to change the subject," Granny said, sitting all the way up, her back against the truck, "but I hear you got yourself suspended. Your daddy called and left a message on my machine, said you'd been fighting." She paused. "Said you wasn't to come over here all week."

"You gonna make me go home?" I asked, knowing the answer already.

"Why? 'Cause your daddy called?" Granny grabbed hold of the door handle and pulled herself up with a grunt. "I don't need him to tell me how to conduct my business with you."

That sounded awful civilized for Granny. She tended to be a little more down in the dirt about her feelings when it came to my dad. The few times I'd seen them in the same room together since my mom died, Granny had always managed to bring the topic around to how my dad didn't do enough to help my mom get better. "They got doctors all over this country that could've cured that girl," she'd say, pointing a bony finger in Daddy's face. "If you'd had a decent job, decent insurance, she'd still be with us today." Then she'd say something about how it had been a mistake ever to let my mom marry him.

My dad always looked like he was going to haul off and pop her one when she said that, but he never did. He'd usually just growl, "You're a crazy old woman," and stomp out of the room. Sometimes I wondered if he wasn't a little bit right. One afternoon, couple years after she died, I'd taken down my mom's photo albums from her closet. My dad's face was cut out of every picture he'd appeared in. Somehow Granny had snuck into our house and done that, which might add up to crazy in some people's books.

"So how 'bout this boy who jumped in the

fight with you," Granny said after I'd told her what happened to get me suspended. "He a friend of yours?"

"Not really," I said, following Granny to the kitchen door. "He asked me over to his house, though."

Granny turned around and looked at me. "You going?"

I shrugged. "Nah. It's too far. He lives over on that old horse farm, over on Strickland."

"Near the Char-Grill," Granny said, nodding. She went inside, holding the door open for me. The kitchen was cool and dark. It smelled like coffee that had been on the burner all day and the lemon oil Granny rubbed on her cabinets. "I heard they sold that place off bit by bit. Taxes got to be too much for 'em. It ain't but a ten-minute bike ride from here."

"Why would I want to go over to his house?" I asked, moving a stack of newspapers off a chair so I could sit down at the kitchen table. "He just wants to talk about the fight, how he's the one who got Cody Peters laid out flat."

"Person invites you over to his house, you

ought to go, I reckon," Granny said. She handed me a can of Coke. "Show 'em you got manners, at the very least. You don't have to stay but fifteen minutes, make some polite talk, then be on your way."

"You think he's having a tea party over there?"

"You could use a friend," Granny said. "You spend too much time with old women." She started washing her hands at the sink, lathering them up good with dishwashing soap. "Wouldn't hurt you to make the effort for once in your life."

Sometimes you can know things about yourself, and I knew I was looking for an excuse to go over to Henry Otis's house, and I knew Granny would nag me into it. I argued back and forth with her for a few more minutes, then acted like I was giving in. "All right, I'll go," I told her. "Just as soon as school lets out. But he's just wanting to brag on that fight."

Granny grinned and grabbed a dish towel to dry off her hands. "Let him brag, then. Sounds like he saved your behind."

FIVE

It didn't take but fifteen minutes to get over to Henry's house. You just had to be careful riding, because traffic was heavy and tight, and it didn't appear that any of them lame-brain motorists cared if I made it alive or not. I parked my bike by the mailbox and walked down the gravel drive to the front door. First time in a long time I'd gone over to somebody's house. I was feeling nervous about it. I didn't even know what I was supposed to say, like what reason was I there for? I was worrying this over and hadn't even knocked yet when Henry opened the door.

"I come to see the chickens," is what I decided on for my opener.

"You've come to the right place," is what he replied.

Out back of Henry's house was a barn and some sheds, and a chicken coop that you could tell was new. As soon as we got a few feet from it, the chickens caught wind of us and started walking in our direction.

"They want to know if we've got food," Henry explained. "To them, the world's one big chicken restaurant and we are merely waiters."

He was wearing his usual baggy outfit, only this time the shirt he had on was like an auto mechanic's, with a little white badge over the left pocket that said DEXTER.

"Your name ain't Dexter," I said, poking my fingers through some chicken wire.

He nodded. "Sure, but maybe it was in another life."

I considered this for a second. "You think you were wearing that shirt in your other life?"

"Wouldn't surprise me," Henry said. "It's a pretty cool shirt."

Then he pointed to the birds squawking

near our feet. "So, what do you think about my chickens?"

I couldn't hardly tell Henry the truth, that his chickens gave me the creeps. Well, I'd always had mixed-up feelings about chickens, and not only from seeing Granny kill some. It was how they moved, their heads going back and forth that way. There's something sort of lizardy about a chicken. Prehistorical, I guess you'd call it, like they don't quite belong in the modern world. Maybe I felt the same way myself sometimes, but that didn't mean I was going to start buddying up with a bunch of birds.

"They're pretty, huh?" Henry nodded to a chicken over in the corner. "Just got her the other day. She's a silver-laced wyandotte."

He walked past the gate into the yard and picked up the chicken. It really did look like it had silver lace over its feathers. "Zuzu, zuzu, shooby dooby," he cooed at it. "Zuzu, zuzu, zuzu."

I looked down at my feet, embarrassed. For me or Henry, or for the chicken, I wasn't quite sure. Maybe all three of us. "Is that some kind of chicken talk?" I asked, wishing like anything that I was home watching TV.

Henry stroked the bird's feathers and looked into its little beady eyes. "I don't know. I guess. It's just what I say to old Zelda here. She likes it." He motioned me to come in. "I'll give you the tour."

The coop looked like a little house. Plywood walls, wood floors, a foot-high door for the chickens to get in and out of, a little ramp leading to the yard. There were windows, and little holes cut out near the tops of the walls, which Henry said were for ventilation, and a door for people to get in and collect the eggs and clean things out. Inside there were nesting boxes for the chickens to lay their eggs in. It wasn't anything like Granny's. She had a bunch of chicken wire stapled to a couple of upright two-by-fours outside an old woodshed in the way back of her yard. The chickens stayed in the shed at night and pecked around in the dirt outside during the day.

Henry's chickens, all five of them—the silver-laced wyandotte, two Rhode Island Reds, a golden-laced wyandotte, and a white leghorn, according to Henry—followed us through their little yard, stopping every second or two to peck at the ground.

"Me and my brother built this place," Henry told me, thumping a wall. "We got books out of the library and drew up plans. My dad helped." Henry grinned. "He helped a lot, if you want to know the truth. I'm not a very good carpenter."

I pictured Henry and his dad and his brother hammering nails and whistling some chirpy song. I could just about hear Patrick snort, "Boy Scout." That's what he said when somebody was too good to be true. He made it sound like he had a bunch of gunk in his throat that he was about to spit out.

"My dad works road construction," I said out of nowhere. "That road in front of your house? He built it."

That was a lie, son. My dad had been working on the 540 beltway since the beginning of time. I just felt like saying something about how my dad built stuff too, even if it wasn't stuff he built with me.

"Oh, yeah?" Henry sounded all polite about it, like he was interested. "That's cool."

"Cooler than this old chicken coop," I muttered. I stood there feeling prehistoric as a chicken. Just from this little thing of the chicken coop being built by Henry and his dad. I didn't understand it at all.

"Yeah, I mean, a road's really important." Henry seemed like he was fishing for the right thing to say. "You must be really proud of your dad."

Now, to show you how all over the place I was, when Henry said that, I got this big feeling in my chest I got sometimes when I thought about my dad. So now I had the big-chest feeling on top of the Boy Scout–snort feeling and the prehistoric-chicken feeling. You can bet I was ready to go home, son, my head was spinning so bad. But just as I was trying to figure a way out of there, this little kid came flying through the backyard, waving a clipboard at us. "You didn't take the eggs, did you?" he yelled, and at first I thought he was yelling at me, like I was some famous egg thief.

"Calm down, Harrison," Henry said as the kid skidded to a halt in front of us. "We didn't get the eggs yet. You can still do your tallies."

Harrison took a second to catch his breath. He fanned himself with his clipboard. You could tell him and Henry were brothers. They both had that color of hair that's not quite blond and not quite brown—wheat colored, I guess you'd call it. And they had brown eyes that almost looked Chinese. Henry was a lot taller and more filled out than Harrison. On the other hand, Harrison's clothes pretty much fit him, and he wore his shirt tucked in.

"Who are you?" he asked me when he could talk again. "And how come you're wearing jeans when it's so hot outside?"

I looked down at my Levi's. I'd been wearing them ever since I got all those remarks about my bird legs in gym. It wouldn't have been so bad if I didn't hear "bawk, bawk, bawk" in my own head every time I caught a glimpse of my knees. No way I was going to say all that to Harrison, though. "I don't know, just am," is what I told him.

"Oh," he said, like that was a good enough answer for him. He stuck out his hand for me to shake. "I'm Harrison Otis. What you need to know about me is that I'm nine years old, I'm going to have a big chicken business one day, and I'm going to run in the Olympics."

I nodded at him, like I thought he had a good plan. He eyeballed me for a couple seconds, looking me up and down. It felt pretty weird to be checked out by a little kid. I mean, he couldn't have been more than four and a half feet tall.

"You up for a race?" Harrison tossed his clipboard down on the ground. "You look like you might be sort of fast."

I felt something going on behind me, and when I turned around, Henry was shaking his head so hard you had to wonder if he was going to shake it right off of his neck. It was like he was trying to send Harrison a secret message: *Do not ask Tobin to race.* But Harrison didn't get it. "Come on and race me, it'll be fun," he said.

I looked down at my sneakers, which were about to flop apart at the seams any second. Then I looked up at Harrison. "I don't mind to race," I told him. And I almost cracked up seeing Henry about to go *splat* flat in the dirt when he heard that.

SIX

"Where you want to race to?" I asked Harrison, and he pointed to a fence about a hundred yards away. "Henry, you go over and do 'Mark, get set, go,'" Harrison said. He picked up a stick and placed it about five feet from where we were standing. "Here's the starting line."

You could see worry weighing down Henry's shoulders as he trotted off to the fence. I guess he didn't want me to get embarrassed from being no kind of athlete. I looked down at the ground, trying to keep the smile off my face. Didn't nobody know how fast I was, but Henry and Harrison Otis were about to find out.

Henry waved his arms and yelled, "Go!"

and me and Harrison took off. For a little kid, Harrison was fast. I thought he might take me, only he stumbled on a rock and that threw him off his stride. Me, I just kept getting it, feeling my legs clipping faster and faster over the grass. I hit the fence full out and rolled onto the ground. Henry was over my face in a second.

"I don't get it," he yelled, waving his arms around. I couldn't tell if he was excited or mad. "If you can run like that, why don't you dress out for gym?"

I sat up, still breathing too hard to talk. Just shook my head at him.

"Because it's not like you've got to be good at every sport," he went on. "If you're pretty good at one sport, that's cool, you don't have to be great at everything."

I shook my head some more. "I don't dress out," I said when I got my breath. "I got better things to do with my time."

Henry flopped on the ground next to me. Now it was his turn to shake his head. "Sitting on the bleachers every day seems like a waste of

41

time to me, my man. Especially if you're a natural-born athlete."

I felt it again right then, that buzzing feeling going all up and down my back. Not once in my life did I ever think I was a natural-born athlete, even though I'd always been fast. Even in elementary school, I knew I could outrun everyone in my class. But I couldn't work up the energy to show off my speed. I'd never been all that interested in making a big impression on people, up until now. Seemed important that Henry Otis knew there was something I could do good.

But "I ain't got nothing to prove," is all I said to Henry.

Henry tilted his head one way, then the other, like he was weighing out something in his head. "Yeah, okay, sure. I'm not saying that you do. But if you've got a God-given ability, why not use it from time to time?"

I didn't know how to answer that, so I didn't.

This whole time me and Henry were talking, Harrison had been under a tree about ten yards away, where he'd flung himself after the race. Now he came over to where me and Henry were sitting. He put out his hand, handshaking being his family's family tradition. "Good race."

I shook his hand for the second time. "You got a bad break," I told him.

Harrison shrugged. "Bad habit to blame the track," he said. Then he got a panicky look in his eyes. "My clipboard! What did I do with it?" He started off in the direction of the chicken coop, but stopped himself short and turned back toward me. "Hey, are you interested in the chicken business? Because we could use another partner. Think about it."

Off he went flying.

I looked at Henry. "Harrison's obsessed with finding another farmer, as he puts it, to go into business with us," he told me. "My mom put a limit on how many chickens we can have, five tops, which doesn't give you enough eggs to make it worthwhile to sell them."

"I don't know nothing about chickens," I said.

"You could learn. I'll teach you."

Sounded like joining a club to me, son. I shook my head.

Then Henry gave me the look. It was the

cool-eyed stare of someone who was going to get his way. "Listen, Tobin. We've established a lot today. For instance, we've established that chickens like you. On top of that, we've established that you're fast. Who knows what other talents lay hidden inside that skinny exoskeleton of yours—"

I interrupted him. "I didn't see one sign them chickens liked me."

"Liked you?" Henry pounded the grass with his fist. "They loved you, man! You don't know anything about chickens, do you?" He said it like it was a capital offense. Jumping up, he began pacing alongside the fence. "I don't even know where to start. There's so much, so much. It's not even about the chicken business, that's Harrison's deal. It's about the chickens. The chickens, do you hear me, Tobin?"

He turned and started walking toward the house. "I want to see you here tomorrow, three P.M. Bring a notebook." He looked back at me. "Do you have a guitar?"

"No," I said, standing up to follow him. "I got a harmonica, though."

Henry gave a violent shake to his head. "No harmonicas. Chickens hate harmonicas. Guitar music soothes them."

Then he slapped me hard on the back, so hard I nearly fell flat on my face. "Tobin, my man, you are going to learn about chickens. And when you learn about chickens, you will learn about life."

SEVEN

Now that I had to ride the bus to school every day, I had plenty of time to think about all the chicken talk Henry was filling up my head with. He had a whole list of "Theories and Facts About Chickens" that he made me write down. This stuff was like the Bible to him. Riding the bus or sitting in front of the TV, I could flip through the pocket-size notebook I stole out of Summer's desk drawer and study on all sorts of interesting chicken facts. For instance:

1. Chickens are social creatures. You should keep at least three at all times.
2. Do not be surprised to see a chicken

rolling around in the dirt, as if it's having a supreme monkey fit. This is how a chicken gets rid of lice and mites.

3. Chickens with white ears lay white eggs. Chickens with red ears lay brown eggs. Araucana chickens lay green or blue eggs.

4. If you do not give your chickens enough space, light, air, and walking-around room, they will eat one another.

5. Chicken Latin—*Gallus Domesticus*

6. A chicken laying an egg will look like a beach ball about to explode. It will also sing. Do not be alarmed!

7. A chicken will mistake a potato for a rock. Chickens can and should eat rocks (little ones; they help them digest their food). They should not eat raw potatoes! Also avoid avocados, chocolate, and onions.

8. Yes, you can hypnotize a chicken, but why would you want to?

For two weeks, Henry gave me chicken lessons. I picked up stuff pretty quick, quicker than

I thought I would. Maybe if they'd taught about chickens at school, I'd have been more interested.

"Now, your average chicken lays an egg a day during the warm months," was the sort of thing Henry told me as we walked down the hallway from English to Mr. Peabody's second-period science class. "Production lessens in winter. It has to do with the light. A chicken needs at least fourteen hours of light a day to produce an egg. The world record is 364 eggs in 365 days. Black Australorp. They're egg machines, man. That's what they're bred for."

I thought on all that information during class, doodling pictures of eggs on my desk, thinking about how much light we got on a winter's day in Raleigh, North Carolina. I did the figures in my notebook. Started getting light around seven in the morning, and you started losing the light around five. That's ten hours. Not enough. But what if you hooked up your coop with electric lights? I wondered. I drew a picture of a lightbulb next to my figuring.

There were a couple of reasons Henry knew so much about chickens. One was that he thought chickens were the center of the universe. The other was that he was doing an extra-credit project on the inner lives of chickens for science class.

"Mr. Peabody doesn't actually believe that chickens have inner lives," Henry explained to me when we were standing at his locker one morning, waiting for the first-period bell to ring. "According to him, their brains are too small. But he hasn't spent enough time around real, live chickens. If he had, he'd know there's a lot going on inside those little heads of theirs."

I thought about Granny's chickens. You couldn't pay me money to believe them birds had ever thought a thought or felt a single feeling other than a hankering to peck in the dirt for bugs. I'd seen red-tailed hawks out in the woods, and I could imagine they had all sorts of noble ideas. But chickens? Forget it, son.

"You could get extra credit too, if you wanted," Henry informed me. He reached into his locker and pulled out his books for English. "Because I could use a little help with this project. I need a good sample of chickens if this study's going to work. It might be hard to prove chickens have inner lives if you only have five chickens to observe."

"I thought you wanted me to get chickens for the eggs."

Henry slammed closed his locker door. "No, that's what Harrison wants. I want you to get chickens so we can discover their souls."

I stared at him for a few seconds, but I didn't say anything. I was happy to help Henry out with his project, but that didn't mean I had to buy all of his crazy ideas.

"You know," Henry said as we turned the corner to hallway C, "I knew the first time I saw you that you were meant to be one with the chickens."

I looked at him, wondering how he'd come up with that idea. "When did you first see me?"

"You were talking to a police officer out in front of the school," he said. "First day. You were so cool, man. It was like nothing got to you. And then later, you came in late to English and you didn't care that people were giving you a hard time. Me, I would have been bumping heads together."

"How's that make me right for working with chickens?"

Henry slapped me on the back. "Chickens desire coolness in a leader, my man. I've had to learn it the hard way, but you've just got it. I admire that."

I looked at the ground and kept on walking. I could feel a smile about to pop out, but I kept it inside.

Besides learning about chickens, I was learning all kinds of things about Henry. For one example, he was a vegetarian. I found this out one day at lunch when he started poking around at some junk in a little plastic container, grayish white blocks covered in a brown sauce and sesame seeds.

"It's tofu," he told me. "A soy-based protein source. Want to try some?"

I shook my head no. "Looks like rubber," I told him, and that was being polite about it, son.

"Yeah, it sort of tastes that way too," Henry admitted. "But I've got to get protein in my diet, dude, and I don't eat meat."

That threw me. I'd never known anyone not

to eat meat. I ate a hamburger every day for lunch. "Why not? Don't you like how it tastes?"

Henry popped a piece of tofu in his mouth and made a face. "I love how meat tastes. But once I started raising chickens, I couldn't eat chicken anymore. How could I eat something I cared about? Besides, I couldn't kill a chicken. Or a cow or a pig. It doesn't seem right to eat something you wouldn't kill yourself."

"You eat fish?"

"Of course I eat fish. I don't have a problem catching a fish."

"How 'bout cutting its head off?"

Henry pondered this. "Theoretically, I would cut a fish's head off, only whenever I've gone fishing, someone else has done it."

I looked at my hamburger for a second, and then I took another bite. I didn't know if I'd kill a cow or not. I figured I'd keep on eating meat until I decided.

Henry waited for me every day at the cafeteria entrance. And he always set his tray down on a front and center table. "I'm like a chicken, my man," he told me when I said I'd rather eat at my old back corner table, where I used to eat before me and Henry got to be friends. "I need space, air, and light."

"You start eating people otherwise?" I asked him.

Henry laughed and slapped one of his trademark thunderclaps on my back.

Sometimes when we were eating, I could feel people's eyes on me. I could feel their thoughts on me, too, like, *What's Tobin doing with a friend?* I'd mostly gone around by myself until Henry came along. Maybe they were remembering how Henry whupped up on Cody in the gym that day. I bet they couldn't figure old Henry out, the way he'd pounded the king of seventh grade and then taken up with somebody like me.

Me, I was just trying to get used to the idea of eating with somebody where you weren't watching TV. Lucky for me, Henry didn't need much help making conversation.

"Did you ever think that seventh grade is

wasted on seventh graders?" was one topic he brought up when we'd been eating together a couple weeks. By this time, I was used to him coming up with all manner of crackpot subjects to discuss. I leaned back in my chair and waited for whatever came next.

Henry spit out a sunflower-seed shell into his lunch bag. "We ought to be hiking around Europe right now. Do you know one person in seventh grade who can sit still for a forty-five-minute period?"

I thought about how I fidgeted and squirmed my way through every class. "Nope," I told him. "I can't."

"That's right," Henry said. "We need to be on the move, seeing and doing. Hands-on learning, my man. Not just sitting in some boring middle school in the middle of some boring town where nothing happens."

I nodded my head, like I was taking him serious. "So, what do you reckon? Throw all the seventh graders in a big yellow school bus and send 'em over to Paris, France?"

Henry slammed his fist on the table. All

over the cafeteria, heads turned at the sound. "Yes, exactly! Get those suckers out of the house, out of the classroom, and into the big, bad world!"

"But what about the chickens?"

"Huh?"

I sat up in my chair. "Who's gonna take care of your chickens when you're running around Europe?"

Henry waved away my question. "Harrison, of course." Then he leaned forward, like he was gonna tell me a secret. "It was the chickens that got me thinking this way. It was the chickens who made me realize that life is right in front of us, but we just ignore it. All my life I've been eating eggs, right? And eating stuff made with eggs? And, until recently, eating chicken. But until me and Harrison got our own chickens, I'd never seen one up close. I'd been reading about chickens in books since I was two. Chicken Little, Henny Penny, you name it. But I'd never experienced an actual chicken."

"You weren't missing much," I told him.

Henry leaned in closer. "Dude," he said, his

voice almost a whisper. "I was missing *every-thing.*"

Just then Maricruz Garza, a girl from our English class, showed up at our table, interrupting our profound chicken talk. "Hey, guys," she said, bumping her hip against the table. I could smell her skin, a smell like roses and the ocean. Froze me right up. "Henry, I just wanted to tell you that I liked what you said in Miss Thesman's class today, about the 'No man is an island' quote." She turned and gave me a significant look, but I couldn't read what it meant.

Henry thanked her. They smiled at each other. Then Maricruz said she had to go. But before she did, she leaned toward me and touched her fingers to my arm. Just left them there for a second, then stood up and said bye.

I didn't know how to read that, either. But my arm tingled and burned for the rest of the afternoon.

EIGHT

"You've got to get at least one Australorp, for maximum eggage," Harrison told me on the day we finally got down to making business plans. We were sitting at the table in the middle of the Otises' blue-and-white kitchen. Harrison kept reading from the notes clamped on his clipboard, stuff about how we were going to make millions of dollars off of a bunch of whizzle-necked birds.

"I don't think egg production should be our main concern right now," Henry said, shoving half of a peanut-butter sandwich into his mouth. About a thousand crumbs spilled down his chin onto the table. "It's almost winter. We're not going to be seeing as many eggs."

You could tell this worried Harrison from a businessman's angle. "That's why Tobin invests in an Australorp," he insisted. "It'll give us a fighting chance to make a profit before spring."

"Me, I want one of them chickens that lays the blue and green eggs," I said, even though I was still nervous about hanging around chickens full-time. What I liked best about the chicken business so far was sitting in Henry's kitchen, everything clean and shiny, the September sun streaming through the window, and all kinds of food just waiting to be eaten. Sometimes after I'd spent an afternoon at Henry's, I could hardly make myself walk through the door to my house. I knew the refrigerator would be empty, and more likely than not I'd be the only one there. I'd go rattling from room to room, turning on TVs and radios, just to feel like I had some company. Going from Henry's house to mine was like walking out of a color movie into one that was nothing but black and white.

"Araucana," Harrison said, making a check on his clipboard. "That's doable."

Henry's mom wandered in to make a cup

of that tea that smelled like strawberry jam. As usual, she was wearing sweatpants and a baggy T-shirt and moccasins, which she joked was her work uniform, since she worked at home editing some magazine about art that people made from glass.

She looked surprised to see me, the way she always did when she walked into the kitchen, but after half a second she got a big smile on her face. "Those blue eyes, Tobin," she said, pouring boiling water from the kettle into her mug. "With that black hair. Be still my heart."

"Mom!" Harrison said, sounding worried. "What about Dad?"

Mrs. Otis made a face. "Dad needs to take out the trash."

Our plan was that once we got our flocks settled, maybe we'd try to add on, if we could convince Henry's mom to let them get more hens. Me, I had to check with my dad to see if I could get some chickens in the first place.

Saturday morning was the best time to talk to my dad. He worked all week, didn't get home until late each night, and he spent most of the weekend at my uncle Rob's house up on the Neuse River. They'd go fishing or Jet Skiing or ride around on Uncle Rob's ATV nine, ten months out of the year. Most of the time he spent Saturday night over there, so if you needed to talk to him, Saturday morning was it.

He was sitting on the couch watching NASCAR news on sports TV and drinking coffee out of the NC State Wolfpack mug that only he was allowed to drink from. I sat on the arm of the couch and waited for a commercial, since you didn't want to get in between my dad and anything having to do with stock-car racing. Finally an ad for underarm deodorant rolled onto the screen, and I got a chance to tell him my plan.

"What you want chickens for?" he asked, taking a swig of coffee after he'd heard me out. "They get all in your business if you're not careful. I know somebody who kept chickens, they damn near took over his house, roosting in the oven and up in the closets."

"I wouldn't keep 'em inside. I'd build a coop, make sure they didn't get out."

My dad raised an eyebrow. "I've been after

60

Shane for a year now to move all them auto parts out of the backyard, and he hasn't lifted a finger. You think you're man enough to make him do it?"

I leaned forward and put my elbows on my knees. I hadn't thought my dad would care, since he was hardly ever there. "I can make room. It's only five chickens."

Daddy turned his eyes back to the television. "Do you even know what the zoning laws are around here?"

This was turning out to be harder than pulling a hair out of an old man's nose. "No," I said, not adding that I wasn't a lawyer, so how could he expect me to know that? "But if it's legal to raise chickens here, can I do it?"

Daddy shook his head and picked up the remote to change the channel. "Look around here, son, and tell me what you see. One mess piled on top of another. Last thing we need is chickens."

I looked around the room. I saw old sneakers and an army of unwashed socks. A trail of empty pizza boxes ran from the couch to the garbage bag that we used for kitchen trash, but not one of them had made the jump inside. The top of the TV appeared to be Summer's makeup storage area. Dust bunnies were peeking out from underneath all the furniture.

I didn't have to go into the kitchen to know it wouldn't pass a health inspection. The bathroom down the hallway would probably get us the wrecking ball if any city official dropped by and heard nature's call while he was here. It was a mess, all right, but I didn't see what difference a few chickens would make. It'd be like adding another dog to Granny's pack.

That gave me an idea. "You care if I do it over at Granny's? She's already got a couple chickens there."

Daddy started flipping past channels, going so fast there was no way he could tell what was on each one. His eyes narrowed, the way they always did when the topic of Granny came up. "You know, I can't for the life of me figure out why you spend so much time over there. Why you want to hang out with that crazy old lady for? All she'll do is talk your ear off."

"She ain't so crazy."

"She's pretty crazy. Do you know she called me last week to see if I'd give her some of the clothes in your mama's closet? Said she knew somebody who'd cut 'em up into squares and make a damn quilt. Said those clothes belonged to her as much as to me. 'Hell no,' is what I told her. That crazy old bat. And she talks all the time, you got to admit it. She talked your grand-daddy to death. The doctor called it a heart attack, but soon as I heard he was dead, I knew that he'd finally taken all he could take of that woman's mouth and just exploded."

Daddy finally landed back at the NASCAR news, where they were showing a race from the week before. He kicked his feet up on the table, his big yellow work boots hitting it with a loud thump. It was like all this time I'd been talking to Daddy from the sidewalk, him in his car, the motor idling, and now it was time for him to roll up his window and drive on. I clawed around in my mind for something else to say.

"I'm doing an extra-credit project in science,"

is what I came up with. I wasn't a hundred percent sure he'd care.

Daddy turned and looked at me, his eyebrows raised, like I'd given him a good surprise. "Really? You?"

I nodded. "That's what the chickens are for. My extra-credit project."

Daddy punched down the volume on the TV a notch. "Well, that's just fine, son." He leaned back against the couch, seeming to think about something. Finally he said, "It's okay if you want to raise chickens over at your granny's. Her kind of crazy ain't the kind that rubs off."

He picked up the remote and hit the volume again. The noise of the engines came up so loud I could practically smell the fumes come out from the TV. That window was going up again fast, I could feel it, but I heard Daddy mutter, "Extra credit. That's good, that's real good," before it closed all the way.

NINE

Granny had one condition before she'd agree to let me use her coop for some chickens. She wanted to meet Henry first. She made it sound like there was some test she was going to make him go through before she'd get involved in any sort of chicken business with him, but she was just curious about him.

So Monday after school me and Henry rode our bikes over to Granny's house. Her dogs came out to meet us when we turned onto the gravel drive. They started wailing, and that racket brought Granny to the front door.

"Hush, all of you, or I'll call animal control on your mangy hides," she yelled, and then she saw us. "You boys sure did start up a commotion."

Granny was too busy drying her hands off with a dish towel and yelling at her dogs to give us a big welcome. "Well, what you waiting for?" she called. "Come on into the house. They got a fishing show on the sports channel. You boys might learn something."

We hopped off our bikes and headed for the door. "You ain't allergic to dogs, are you?" I asked Henry.

"No, not the last time I checked."

"That's probably a good thing," I said, and I was right, because the second Henry stepped through the door, he was knocked flat by the biggest dog in Granny's pack.

"Yeah, that's probably a real good thing," I repeated, and then I about bust a gut laughing when the stupid dog started licking Henry to death.

"Calvin, get off that boy, now, get off him." Granny grabbed the monster by his collar. "He won't bite you. He just wants to love on you a little bit. Why don't you go sit down on the couch, and I'll throw Calvin outside."

The summer before seventh grade I had spent a part of nearly every day over at Granny's, sprawled across the same yellow-and-brown plaid couch Henry was sitting on now. I took a seat next to him and looked around, trying to see Granny's house from a stranger's eyes. Piles of newspapers leaned against the water-stained walls, and boxes of canning jars were jammed into the corners. Everywhere you could see there was fishing tackle and fishing poles and line. I popped my feet onto the big spool table in front of the couch and nearly knocked a pile of *Outdoor Life* magazines to the floor.

If Henry lifted his head and looked down the hallway, he wouldn't see much, just three closed doors. One was to Granny's room, which she kept private and off-limits. One was to the bathroom. Across from Granny's room was the door to my mom's room from when she was growing up. Whenever I stayed overnight, that's the room I slept in. Wasn't much in there, a bed and a bunch of boxes filled with old clothes, a few posters on the wall. But I liked scrambling under the sheets and the old checkered bedspread and getting the feel of having a room to myself. I liked waking up in the morning and knowing Granny would whip me up some breakfast, cereal mostly, but sometimes eggs or pancakes.

Granny came back in and caught Henry eye-balling her prize possession. "That's my fly-making machine," she told him. "I like to tie my own flies. What they got over there at the Kmart's junk, pure T junk. Couldn't catch a cold with them Kmart flies. You like to fish, son?"

She sat down in her old brown recliner chair and kicked back, looking at Henry the whole time, like she expected a good answer from him. Her little toes were poking out of her navy blue Keds sneakers.

"Right at the beginning of summer," Henry told her. "That's the best fishing time for me, when we go up to the mountains to see my grandparents. There's a good creek across the street from their place. Me and my dad catch a lot of sunfish there."

Granny nodded. Her bright blue eyes looked at Henry straight on. "Some good creeks around here. 'Course, lot of them fish is dying off.

Pollution and all. Now, the thing I like is to drive down to Morehead City when I get a chance and do some bridge fishing. You just sit on a bridge and cast off. I see a lot of the same folks every time I go down there. 'Willa,' they say to me, 'we was just talking about you.' Every time I go, they say that. Now, how can that be, you reckon?"

"Maybe it's just something people say," Henry said, and she nodded.

"That's what I was thinking. Else it's ESP. You believe in that?"

"I don't know. Maybe."

"They say it's of the devil, so it's best not to fool around with it," she warned.

Didn't look like Henry knew how to answer that, so he just nodded.

"Now, Tobin's mama, she liked to fish," Granny said, going back to her original topic. "His mama, Sandy, she was my girl. She took after me, and Tobin takes after her. Almost five years gone, if you can believe it. Cancer. It ate her right through, the way it'll do some folks. You know anybody to die of cancer?"

Henry shook his head no.

"Terrible thing," she said. "Terrible thing."

Henry looked over at me, but I had my eyes glued to the fishing show like I wasn't even listening to the conversation.

"I'm glad to see Tobin's got himself a friend. He's been needing one. Him and his mama was close. She taught him how to fish. I taught her, she taught him. That's how families work, son. You pass things on."

Granny turned and studied the TV for a minute. "I hate bass fishing. Bass are stupid fish. Lot of smart fish out there, but a bass ain't one of 'em."

The next thing we knew, she was hustling out glasses of sweet iced tea and a box of saltine crackers from the kitchen and arranging everything on the spool table. "You boys ought to eat something now. Boys need to eat."

She took a swig from her own tea glass before popping back down in her recliner. "You live out on that farm on Strickland?" When Henry nodded, she said, "Me, I'd rather fish than farm. I grew up on a farm, and my first husband was a farmer, but after a while I just got tired of all the dirt. You that way? You ever get tired of dirt? Me, I got real tired of it. Red dirt, black dirt, it makes no difference to me. If I didn't have to, I wouldn't even put in a garden, but a body's got to eat, and I like tomatoes in the summer. Ain't a tomato worth eating to be bought from a grocery store. They's all cardboard. Them stores ought to be ashamed to sell 'em. Only, nobody's ashamed of nothing anymore, are they?"

"Granny, you talk too much," I said, not bothering to take my eyes off of the TV screen. "I ain't never heard no one talk as much as you. Teachers don't talk as much as you do, and they don't do nothing but talk all day."

"What'd you bring this boy over here for if you didn't want me to talk to him?"

I shrugged. "You asked me to bring him to meet you."

"That's right, I did," Granny said. "Ain't no one else in your family worth meeting. Not your daddy, nor that Patrick or Shane, nor that sister of yours. I'm all you got that's worth meeting."

I kept watching the TV. "You ever get a hook

71

stuck in you?" I asked Henry, wanting to change the topic. "I did once, right in my earlobe."

"Your mama was fit to be tied," Granny said. "How old were you, Toby? Seven?"

"Six," I told her. "Mama said I was lucky it didn't pluck my eye out."

It was funny talking about that. Long time since I'd remembered things from when my mom was still alive. It made me feel sad, but at the same time I wanted to talk about it some more, look it over from all sides, see if I could catch a picture of Mama's face in my mind.

"She hated for anything bad to happen to you," Granny said. "Didn't ever want to hear you cry. I never saw someone spoil a baby so."

Then she put down her tea glass. "All right then, boys. Tell me about this chicken business. I'd like to know what I'm getting myself into."

Walking out to our bikes, Henry started shaking his head, like he'd just seen something he couldn't believe. "Your grandmother's really cool. There's not one person in my family who's remotely as cool as your grandmother. My grandparents live in Florida, except for in the summer when they stay in this stuffy mountain resort. They golf constantly. I bet nobody in your family golfs."

That about cracked me up. Closest anybody in my family ever got to a golf course was when Shane and his buddies decided to hold a midnight barbecue over at the North Raleigh Country Club. Daddy had to go down to the police station at 3 A.M. to bail Shane out.

"Can't say I've ever heard of any golfers related to me," I told him, swinging a leg over my bike and pushing off toward the road. "Just race car fans and fishermen."

"Well, a fish is much cooler than a golf ball," Henry said, following me up the driveway. "It's not as cool as a chicken, but it beats a golf ball by a mile."

Hard to argue with that, son.

TEN

The next Saturday me, Henry, and Granny went to get my chickens. It was the first week of October, and Granny had just gotten her driver's license back, so she was ready to lay a little rubber to the road. Said she knew somebody who knew somebody who had a variety of laying hens he was willing to sell, out at a farm on old Highway 98, going into Durham. No Australorps, but he did have an Araucana and two Rhode Island Reds and two white leghorns, all under two years old, meaning that they still had some good egg-laying days ahead of them. Me, Henry, and Harrison had pooled our money to pay for them, Harrison making it clear that he was investing in the business and would expect to get his investment back as soon as we turned a profit.

"First thing we do when we get there is listen," Henry said in the truck on the way over. "If the chickens aren't making noise, we don't want them."

"Why not?" I fiddled with the radio, trying to get a song that Granny could live with, which meant something country or nothing at all.

Henry tapped the side of his head. "Mental health in a chicken is very important, my man. We want happy, talkative chickens. If the coop is quiet, turn tail and run."

I landed on a song about daddies and pickup trucks and Fourth of July parades, which was right up Granny's alley. "What else, Mr. Chicken Expert?"

"Bright eyes. Good poop."

"We got to check their poop?"

Henry looked at me like, how could I ask such a dumb question? "Poop is at the top of the list of things to check. You need to see high-quality poop coming out of a chicken's rear end before you buy it. No diarrhea. Nothing funky."

Granny was nodding. "You can tell a lot about an animal by its bowel movements. You want to look at its eyes, too. My second husband brought home a sick pig once. I knew it the minute I looked at her. Eyes were dull as dirt. Normally a pig is a real bright-eyed creature, but this one looked like it'd been watching TV and drinking all afternoon. Made the other pigs sick, too."

"I'll check out the eyes," I told Henry. "You can be in charge of the poop."

Granny turned off the highway onto a gravelly lane. "Make sure they ain't too henpecked, neither. You don't want one at the bottom of the pecking order, that's what I've always been told. Them's the ones too nervous to lay regular."

Mr. Bynum Nelson was the man selling the chickens. He walked us down to his coop, past a pigpen that seemed to hold as many geese as pigs. "I never did see such pigs for loving geese," Mr. Nelson said as we passed by. "Only, they're bad for eating the eggs."

"Good-looking pigs," Granny remarked,

"real healthy." That seemed to please Mr. Nelson. His cheeks went red and he gave a wave of his hand, saying, "We do our best to take care of 'em."

You'd think there was some sort of chicken party going on, for all the racket we heard coming up to the coop. I looked at Henry. He gave me the thumbs-up sign. As soon as we saw the birds, he got this glow about him, like he'd entered chicken heaven as the guest of honor. As Mr. Nelson pulled out the chickens he was wanting to sell, Henry nodded his head, slow at first, and then faster.

"You having a seizure?" I asked him. "Or you just seeing better poop than you expected?"

"These are fantastic chickens," Henry said, grinning. He held out his arms and turned around in a circle, like he was taking it all in. "It's great to be here. Real chickens, real pigs, real geese. This is where it all begins."

"Where what begins?"

"Real life, man. Unprocessed, unpackaged. It's not TV, it's not some video about farms you watched in second grade. It's the real thing."

Mr. Nelson stood behind Henry, holding a wire cage filled with five chickens. "You one of them organic types?" he asked, sounding suspicious. "Let your chickens roam hither and yon?"

"Yep," Henry answered him. "No growth hormones, no antibiotics, and they're free to roam the roost."

"It figures." Mr. Nelson stepped around Henry and headed toward Granny's truck. "Good luck with the coryza, that's all I gotta say."

I turned to Henry. "What's coryza?"

"Chicken disease, lots of eye pus involved," Henry informed me. "Not a problem if you don't let your chickens get stressed out. A relaxed chicken is a healthy chicken, remember that."

Nobody'd said anything to me about chicken diseases. All the talk about poop was bad enough. "You gonna come back with me to Granny's?" I asked Henry as we drove away from the farm, gravel crunching under the truck's tires. I wasn't sure I wanted to be left alone with my new chickens now that I had eye pus to worry about.

He shook his head. "It's got to be you and

78

those chickens at first. You've got some serious bonding to do. You might try singing to them."

We dropped Henry off at his house before driving the chickens back to Granny's. The chickens would stay in the shed until me and Henry could build something better. We didn't have to worry about introducing my new flock into Granny's old flock. She'd eaten the last of her chickens for supper the Sunday before, to make room.

Granny helped me get the chickens out of the cage and into the coop. Then she went inside to do chores. I had a tube feeder and a waterer already set up, and I'd put out some crushed-up oyster shells in a pie plate so the chickens would get plenty of calcium for strong eggshells.

The chickens pecked around in the dirt in the yard. I was used to chickens by now, after all my training with Henry, but I still didn't feel friendly toward them. Not the way Henry did with his chickens. If Henry had come over, he'd have hugged on these chickens and looked 'em in the eye and said, "Zuzu, zuzu." He'd have come up with a bunch of good chicken talk to get everybody relaxed.

Well, that was the difference between me and Henry right there. He was a talker and I wasn't. He talked to the cafeteria ladies when he bought his milk for lunch, and he talked to the kids at the tables around us when we ate. He talked in class until the teacher shut him up. Henry was a world-class talker, which made me a world-class listener. But when I listened to the chickens, I couldn't understand a thing they were trying to tell me.

"Maybe I oughta name you," I said to the chickens. That could be step one of my scientific process, seeing if the chickens cared whether or not you called them by name. The Araucana looked at me with an orange eye. Her head moved back and forth in that chicken way. "I'm gonna call you Miss Blue," I told her. "Since that's the color of your eggs." She didn't say a word, but it seemed like maybe she halfway understood what I was saying.

I named one of the Rhode Island Reds Rufus, since I knew *rufus* had to do with some kind of red animal. Maybe a red dog, but a chicken wouldn't know that. I named the one that scratched the dirt with her left foot Lefty. The white leghorns were Willie, after Granny, and Otis, after Henry. I told them their names over and over so they could learn them. Then I tried to figure out what I should do next. When I got tired of just standing there gawking at the chickens, I sat down in the dirt.

Out of nowhere I started humming "This Land Is Your Land." Miss Blue walked right over to me. She cocked her head to the left and then to the right. She acted like it was a familiar song to her. For a minute I thought she might start singing with me, but after a couple of verses she went on her way, bobbing her head. I didn't know if that bird had a soul or not, but I was pretty sure she had a brain, and I guessed that was a start.

ELEVEN

The sun got low in the sky, and I decided to head home on my bike. Saturday night, so who knew what I could round up for dinner. Summer'd worked the lunch shift at O'Brien's, the restaurant where she waitressed, so maybe she'd brought something home in one of them clear plastic boxes, leftover hamburgers from the lunch rush, chicken-fried steak and fries, something like that.

When I got home, my brother Shane was sitting in front of the TV watching an NC State football game. He grunted "hey" at me when I walked through the front door.

"Summer get home from work yet?" I asked

him, getting hungrier and hungrier the more I thought about the might-could-be chicken-fried steak in the fridge.

"Nah," Shane said, not taking his eyes off the screen. "She called to say she was working a double shift. If some guy named Ray calls, she says to be sure to tell him that."

There wasn't a crumb of something to eat in the kitchen. "You got money for a pizza?" I yelled to Shane, even though I could have told you the answer without waiting to hear it. Shane had a part-time job over at Home Depot, but his pockets must've had holes in them, because he was always flat broke.

"Nope, I ain't got a dime," Shane called from the living room. "Becca's coming by later to take me to Mickey D's."

I turned full around in the kitchen, halfway wanting to cry from being hungry and from the mess of it all. You ought to be able to come into your kitchen and just grab yourself a bite to eat, the way we could at Henry's. You could walk into Henry's house and the dishes were clean and in the cupboard. They had a pantry where you could find three kinds of bread and five different brands of crackers. Cookies, at least two kinds. And if you couldn't find what you wanted, you know what you did? You called upstairs to Henry's mom, and she'd come help find what you were looking for or the next-best thing to it.

I picked up a dish from the counter. I was thinking about smashing it just because nothing in my house was the way it should be. Instead I did something that you'd never believe. I started washing it.

I didn't even know how to wash a dish. It wasn't like anyone around my house had been giving lessons. I grabbed the dried-up old sponge that had been sitting on the windowsill and held it under the faucet until it fattened up with water. Then I started scrubbing it across the plate. I got the crud off of the plate, but when I held it up to the light, it still didn't look all that clean.

"You got to use soap," Shane said from the doorway. "And hot water, too."

"You an expert or something?" I gave the plate another scrub.

"I sort of am now," he said, grinning. "Becca makes me do dishes all the time when I stay over there."

My brother Shane was six foot four inches tall with shoulders the size of a minivan. It about cracked me up imagining him in an apron in front of a sink, little bubbles dancing around his head. Granny was always saying that Shane had rocks for brains. Maybe it was soap bubbles up there instead.

"What you doing them dishes for, anyway?" Shane asked. "Summer'll do 'em tomorrow probably, if she ain't working."

"I figured if I maybe washed a dish, then some food might magically appear on it. Looks like magic is the only thing that's gonna get me fed tonight."

Shane came over to the sink and twisted the faucet to the hot side. "Give me that sponge. The way you're doing it, you'll end up with magic dog food on that plate. Find a dish towel to dry. You know how to dry a plate? It's sort of like drying your backside after you take a shower."

I had to go get a towel from under the

bathroom sink. Shane handed me a wet plate when I got back, and said, "I bet Becca will buy you a hamburger from McDonald's. Pitiful, starving children make her cry."

I rubbed the towel around the plate. I dried five more the same way before we heard Becca's horn blasting out front. I looked around the kitchen. Five dishes didn't make a dent in that mess, son. Made me mad I'd even tried to make things better, when it would take a hurricane to sweep it all away so you could start over from the beginning.

"You coming?" Shane called, heading out the front door. I didn't answer. I was thinking about Henry, how him and Harrison were probably sitting down to eat at that very second, their mom and dad putting food on the table, everybody smiling, music playing in the background, not the TV. They'd probably have some interesting conversation about what big family project they were going to do next.

"Boy Scout," I snorted, but my heart wasn't really in it.

"What'd you say?" Shane yelled, but I was too

busy hustling into my jacket to reply. I left through the back door, picked up my bike off the driveway, and pedaled as hard as I knew how back to Granny's. I was hitting rocks in the road on purpose so the outside of me would feel the same as the inside, all sharp edged and dangerous.

"Calm down there, son," Granny said when I slammed into the kitchen. "Get yourself something to eat. All I got is hot dogs, but they're warm in the pot and you're welcome to 'em."

I threw my jacket on a pile of newspapers. "I think it's time I came and lived with you," I announced. Didn't even know it was true until I said it, and then I realized that's what I'd been wanting for a long time. "You've got the room, and I need me a place to stay."

Granny plucked a hot dog out of the pot with her fingers, let the water drip off for two seconds, and dropped it into a bun. "You got a place to stay over where you live. What you want to set up camp with an old woman for?"

"Better than living at that dump. Can't get a decent meal there to save your life. And nobody's ever home. You could starve to death, they wouldn't find your body for days. I'd be a lot better off over here."

"I'd hate for you to starve to death, now that's true," Granny said. She handed me the hot dog on a paper towel, then opened the refrigerator and pulled out a bottle of ketchup. "But I'm too set in my ways, son. And I snore like a freight train, so I'm told. I think we got us a good arrangement like it is, me driving you to school again. You're already here half the day. I need the other half to myself. I been through two husbands and Lord knows how many boyfriends. I need some peace now and then."

She handed me the bottle of ketchup. "You're coming to me in my worn-out days. Ten years ago I mighta done it, but not now."

Once, when I was around nine, I got beaned in the head with a baseball. You know what that's like, getting hit in the head? It takes your brain a few seconds to figure out what just happened, because that kind of pain is the last thing in the world it expects. Same way when Granny said she didn't want me to live with her. I sat there a minute with my mouth half stuffed with hot dog, words swirling around between my ears, all scrambled up into nonsense.

And then the words sank in and so did the hurt, going deep into places I didn't even know could hurt just from somebody saying they didn't want you.

"It don't matter," I mumbled, squishing the tail end of my hot-dog bun into a little ball. "I'm fine where I am." I tried hard to sound like that was true. But if it was so true, why'd I want to curl up under the table and bawl my eyes out?

Granny passed behind my chair and gave me a squeeze on the back of my neck, the closest thing she had to a hug. "I'm no picnic, son," she said, like that was supposed to make me feel better.

But you're all I got, I thought and walked over to the stove for something else to eat.

TWELVE

The next Monday my name was on the board in Miss Thesman's room. Me, Jarvis Keller, and Sara Leever were the only three who hadn't turned in our autobiographies yet. When Henry saw that, he about bust a gut.

"We're not doing anything until you get that done. No coop building, no science projects, nothing," he told me as we walked out of English.

"Why do you care? You ain't the one that's gonna get an F."

"Because," he said, and I knew he didn't have an answer, just a feeling. He started fishing around for what he wanted to say. "You like Miss Thesman, right?"

I shrugged. "I like her well enough."

That made Henry laugh. "You nearly got yourself killed over her. You were her knight in shining armor, my man, and that is why you have to finish this paper."

"Why?"

"Because you can't get your butt kicked over a woman and then not do your homework for her," Henry said, having finally figured out his thinking. "Where's the honor in that?"

"I can't write an autobiography. There ain't nothing to write about. I got some facts written down, but nothing worth reading. Who cares if my favorite color's blue?"

"Dude," Henry said, shaking his head. "I've met your grandmother. You've got plenty to write about."

That afternoon I sat in Henry's kitchen, notebook open in front of me, twisting and twirling a felt-tip pen around in my fingers. I couldn't think of a word to write.

"You could start with seeing your grandmother twist off a chicken's head with her bare hands," Henry said. "That sounds like a formative experience."

Harrison, who was standing behind him drinking a glass of milk, went pale. "Your grandmother did what?"

"That ain't an autobiography," I said. "That's just an old story about something my granny did."

"You were there, weren't you?" Henry asked. "You saw what happened, which means it happened to you, right? That means it's autobiography."

"I can't write about that in a paper for school."

"Miss Thesman didn't say you couldn't write about chickens. All she said was there were no rules, except it had to be at least five typewritten pages, double-spaced."

"You write it," I said. "I'll tell you what to write down. It takes me so long to write anything, the words all fall out of my head before I get 'em put on the paper."

Harrison walked over to the counter and picked up his clipboard. "I can write it. I write cursive really fast. Then later Henry can help you type it on our mom's computer."

"Okay," I said. "Well, write down that thing about Granny and the chicken, then."

"You've got to tell it to me," Harrison said. "It's got to be in your own words exactly. And you need to think about some other stories that happened to you, too."

"I'm just doing one story today. Maybe I'll do another one tomorrow."

That was Monday. Every day after that I told one more story, and Harrison wrote it down. Me, Henry, and Harrison sat in the kitchen after we put the new eggs in the refrigerator for Henry's mom to use for cooking and hosed down the coop. Henry pulled out his homework, and Harrison pulled out his clipboard, and I drank milk and ate peanut-butter sandwiches and told a story. Tuesday I told about the time in third grade I fell off the monkey bars and broke my arm. Wednesday's story was about how my mom used to grow pumpkins in our backyard. One year Shane got mad because she wouldn't let him go to the movies, and he smashed them all up. Thursday I told dog stories.

"Best dog we ever got was named Scooter," I said, and Harrison's pen started racing across the paper. "Just some mutt Daddy got from a guy at work who was gonna shoot it."

Harrison stopped writing. "Why? Why was he going to shoot his dog?"

"Didn't want to feed it no more, I guess. Scooter was a yapper, that might have been why."

"That's awful," Harrison said, shaking his head. "Okay, keep going."

"So anyway, Daddy comes home with Scooter, and Mama just goes crazy. We had four dogs already, then. Daddy brung home strays all the time. 'I ain't feeding this dog,' Mama said. 'I ain't in no way, no how, taking care of this dog.' So Daddy handed it to me and said, 'This here's your responsibility, son.' I was only seven, but I took real good care of him."

I took a bite of my sandwich and kept talking. "The best thing about Scooter was he was a fishing dog. You could take him down to the creek and he'd get you a good little fish every time. That's what finally got Mama warmed up to him. 'Scooter, go fetch me some dinner,' she'd say. 'If you can't get a bass, then make it a flounder.'"

Harrison held his right hand up, like a traffic cop saying stop, his other hand still writing. "If you can't get a bass," he said under his breath, writing the words, "then make it a . . .

"What was that again?" he asked, looking up.

"Flounder," I said. "That's a joke, son. You can't catch flounder in a creek."

"Is that it for today?" Harrison asked when he finished writing. "Or is there another story?"

"That's it." I took a long drink of milk. Harrison ripped the page out of the notebook he'd been writing in and added it to the stack in my folder. "You've got a lot of pages now, Tobin," he said.

I reached over and grabbed the folder. "That's pretty cool." I smiled even though I was trying not to. "Pretty cool."

"You want to come over Sunday and type it up?" Henry asked me.

"Nah," I said. "I'll take care of it."

"Don't forget. Why flunk English if you don't have to?"

"I'll take care of it," I repeated. Then I looked over to the counter, where the peanut butter and bread and milk jug were still out. "You think your mom would mind if I made me one more?"

"Go ahead," Henry said. "Make two."

"All right, I will," I said, and I did.

I turned in my autobiography on Friday. I'd stayed up till midnight on Thursday putting all the stories into my own handwriting. Took forever and it looked awful, words slanting this way and that, but it was mine. I couldn't remember the last time I turned in a paper I'd actually worked on. Usually I just copied stuff out of encyclopedias or wrote some mess down so that the teacher'd have an excuse to pass me out of her class.

I felt embarrassed, wondering what Miss Thesman was going to do when I gave it to her. I'd had a teacher in sixth grade, Mrs. Keller, who was about a hundred years old, and whenever I did any work in class, she'd put her hand over her heart and get this big, shiny smile on her face, like I was just the best little boy she'd ever met. Made me want to curl up on the floor and roll away.

Miss Thesman, though, she was a professional. "I'll have to mark it down for lateness," she told me. "And for not being typed." I said I understood.

The morning light streamed in through the windows and made the tops of the desk shine gold. Taking my seat, I could smell perfume and soap and chewing gum all mixed up together in the air. I took out a pencil and a notebook. Not that I planned on doing any extra work, but I wanted to be ready in case I thought of anything else that needed writing down.

THIRTEEN

Miss Thesman gave me a C+ on my autobiography, one grade dropped due to lateness. Then she sent a note home to my dad. It came through the mail the day before Halloween and was sitting there on the kitchen table when Daddy got back from work. He dumped out a bag of McDonald's on a plate and took Miss Thesman's note and his plate over to the couch. First he got himself all balanced, then he opened up the envelope.

"This teacher of yours wants me to come to the open house over at the middle school," Daddy said when he was done reading. "Says you're making impressive gains in her class. That's her words, not mine."

He sat back, took a bite of a Quarter Pounder. "You think I ought to go to this thing?"

I tried to imagine my dad sitting in a desk in Miss Thesman's classroom. I could see his legs sprawling out into the aisle and his back and shoulders all hunched up so that his upper half fit in the seat. Made me nervous just thinking about it. "You wanna go?" I asked.

"Not really," Daddy said, and I was all-over relieved. But after he chewed a bite of his hamburger, he said, "On the other hand, it ain't every day someone sends me a note about one of my children that says they're making impressive gains. Fact is, this is the first time a teacher's bothered to comment on one of my children, at least to say something good. I guess I ought to go and give my compliments to the chef or whatever it is you're supposed to do."

The night of the open house, Daddy took a shower soon as he got home from work. When he walked out of his bedroom, a cloud of piney-smelling aftershave trailing behind him, he was struggling with a red-and-green-striped tie that made him look like Christmas on a stick. "I used to know how to tie one of these things," he complained, "but I got out of practice."

Shane pushed himself up from the couch and said, "I'll get it," and Patrick got to laughing so hard Shane turned red from it. "Becca taught me how for when we go to church," he said, and Patrick laughed even harder.

Summer walked in the front door from work and set out straightaway to fix up Daddy's hair, grabbing a big pink comb out of her purse and fussing over Daddy's head, changing the part, trying to squash down his cowlick, until he snarled, "Quit it already. I'm pretty enough as it is."

Before he left, Daddy leaned this way and that to catch his reflection in the living room's front window. "You look handsome, Daddy," Summer remarked. "You ought to dress up more, get you a suit-and-tie job."

Daddy waved her comments away. "I feel like I'm about to choke to death."

"That's why I hardly ever go to church,"

Shane agreed. "Halfway through I'm like to pass out from the tie."

Me, Shane, Summer, and Patrick were all sitting on the couch like we were waiting for Santa Claus to show up. The TV was on, but we were watching Daddy instead.

"Don't believe everything they tell you," Patrick called after him as he was going out the door. "Only the bad stuff."

Shane leaned over and socked him hard on the shoulder. "Don't ruin it," he said, and I knew exactly what he meant. I couldn't think of the last time everybody in my family was sitting in the same spot doing something other than watching TV, something that everybody was a part of.

Two hours later I was pacing back and forth in front of the TV like I was waiting for a baby to be born. I'd guessed Daddy'd be back in no time flat, forty-five minutes at the most, figuring in driving time. When the front door finally opened around 10 P.M., I nearly fell down on the couch. I felt like I'd been holding my breath the whole time he'd been gone.

"Man, oh man, I hadn't been in a school in

a million years," Daddy said, pulling off the red-and-green Christmas tie and unbuttoning the top three buttons of his shirt. "But the funny thing is, even though that school of yours is as new as morning, it smells exactly like every school I ever went to. Chalk and gym socks, I guess. Teachers' bad breath."

He sat down on the couch, switched on the sports news. "That English teacher of yours likes you. Says you're improving all the time, paying more attention. She thinks you can do even better. Your PE coach don't think much of you, though."

"You saw all my teachers?"

"Yeah, I saw all your teachers. You think I was just going to see the ones that think you're okay? That'd narrow it down to two."

"Who else likes me besides Miss Thesman?"

"That science teacher you got. Mr. Longbody."

"Peabody."

"Yeah, that's right. He's so tall, is what threw me off his name. He says when you do your work, you do good."

Daddy stretched out his legs, kicked off his shoes. "You know, I did good at school."

"You did?"

"Don't act so surprised. Yeah, I did good. Math and science, that was my thing. Couldn't write a sentence to save my life and didn't care to read a book. But numbers and anything that had to do with nature, I liked. I always felt bad that Shane and Summer didn't like school better. I should've made 'em graduate instead of doing GEDs. But your mama was so sick, I couldn't keep on top of everything."

He looked at me. "You think about her much?"

It was the first time I could remember him asking me about my mom. I thought for a minute and shrugged. "Sometimes I do. I don't remember everything about her. Lot of little things, like the way she smelled and how she always said 'howdy' instead of 'hi.' I remember a few stories about stuff she did, like with that fishing dog."

"I remember that dog," Daddy said, grinning. "He yapped so much I wanted to give him back, but Sandy loved it too much by then."

And that was it, end of conversation. But when I got up to go to my room, Daddy patted the couch beside him. "Don't run off," he said. "Have a seat and let's see if I can learn you anything about car racing. About time you studied up on the important stuff."

I sat down next to him. All the sudden I wanted to tell him all sorts of things, like about Henry and the chickens, about Miss Thesman and writing my autobiography, all those old stories I'd pulled out of my head. But it'd been so long since I had any real sort of talk with my dad, I'd forgotten how to go about it.

So I kept my mouth shut. But when he started talking about car racing, pointing out this fact and that one, I listened. I listened as hard as I could.

FOURTEEN

Fall break came the weekend after the open house, one whole Thursday and Friday of freedom plus the weekend. When Granny called to invite me to spend the break with her, it took me thirty seconds tops to stuff a few T-shirts and some clean underwear in my backpack and leave Daddy a quick note on the kitchen table. Maybe she didn't want me living with her, but at least she could stand my full-time company for a few days.

She was cleaning out her refrigerator with paper towels and a spray bottle of ammonia. Granny'd always joked she had one of them self-cleaning refrigerators, but all it took was one peek inside to know she'd made that idea up.

The fact was, Granny's house wasn't a whole lot neater than mine, even if she was better about taking out the trash. It was just friendlier somehow, maybe because she always had a pot of coffee warming on the stove and something for you to eat if you were hungry.

"You can't be too careful about germs these days, what with your *E. coli* and your mad cow disease," she told me when I asked her what the heck she was doing. "Besides, I heard the motor grinding away in the middle of the night last night, and I figured it was working too hard, the way it has to make everything cold through all those layers of crud."

I lugged out a couple bags of slimy lettuce and petrified carrots for her, then helped get dinner ready. What I liked best about eating at Granny's house was she always served you campout-style food—hot dogs or sloppy joes, baked beans and biscuits cooked in a cast-iron pan. Me and Granny liked to talk about how we were going to go camping together one of these days. There was a spot on Jordan Lake, she said, where we could catch fish every morning for our breakfast. "You cast your line out of your tent while you're still in your sleeping bag," she liked to say. "You can catch your breakfast in five minutes."

After I scooped up the last of my baked beans on a biscuit, Granny had another surprise for me. She reached up to the top of the refrigerator and pulled down an apple pie, a real one, not from the frozen-food section of the Food Lion. "Betcha didn't know I could make one of these, did you?" she crowed, dishing out a quarter of the pie onto a plate she then set in front of me on the table. "You might think this old woman don't have any tricks left up her sleeve, but just you wait."

It made me nervous to see Granny acting so strange, cleaning her house and baking pies. Next thing you'd know, she'd be telling me to scrub behind my ears before I went to bed. The rest of the night I couldn't help but feel like something was going to pop out from behind the couch or under the rug. I even kept the light on when I crawled into bed, just in case Granny had some surprise waiting for me in the middle of the night.

The next morning the sound of voices woke

me up. I stumbled down the hallway to the kitchen, where I found Henry sitting at the kitchen table eating a piece of cinnamon toast.

"Dude, it's almost lunchtime," he complained when he saw me. "Are you going to sleep all day or are you going to help me do some chicken work?"

Granny got up to pour herself another cup of coffee. "Your friend here is trying to explain to me how it is that chickens have souls. Now, I'm not a religious woman, but my mama dragged me to church every Sunday from the time I was born till I was eighteen years old and married, and not once did any preacher ever mention anything about the soul of a chicken. I've heard folks argue about whether or not dogs had souls, and if you ask me, they do. But a dog is a dog, and a chicken is a chicken. Two different creatures entirely."

"But a chicken has a brain, right?" Henry leaned back in his chair. You could tell he was enjoying this discussion, the way he was grinning ear to ear. With Granny, Henry had finally met his match for talking and arguing about things.

Granny pushed me down into a chair and

put a box of cornflakes in front of me. She grabbed a bowl and a carton of milk and plopped them next to the cereal. "A chicken's got a couple pieces of gravel up there, that's it. Don't go fooling yourself into believing it's the same thing we got in our heads or a dog's got in its head. A chicken brain is a pebble with a few nerves running out of it."

"Henry, let me ask you something," Granny went on, pulling a spoon from a drawer and handing it to me. "Have you once really and truly looked a chicken in the eye? Son, if you have, you know there ain't nothing there."

"Mrs. Fletcher, I have to respectfully disagree with you. I *have* looked a chicken in the eye, and what I've seen could fill a book. Have you ever played guitar for a chicken? The guitar soothes the chicken's soul. I've seen it happen a million times."

"What you're talking about is the nervous system, son, not the soul!" Granny shook her head and sighed. "You're getting the two things all confused. You could play the guitar for a clam and it'd relax. That's how living things work. A houseplant would probably relax if you played it the right song. They say if you talk to a philodendron, it'll grow better."

"Okay, how about a fish," Henry said. "You like to fish. Do you think fish have souls?"

Granny sat down and took a sip of her coffee. She hummed a little bit so we'd know she was thinking. Finally she said, "Now, I love fish. Lots of fish and me have had good relationships. But no, I don't think a fish has a soul. A dog has a soul, but fish and chickens are soul-free."

"But you just said it yourself!" Henry exclaimed. "You've had relationships with fish. How can you have a relationship with something that has no soul? Do you know that some Native Americans believe that everything has a soul, even trees?"

"I'd believe a tree had a soul before I believed a chicken had one," Granny said, nodding, like there was finally something she and Henry agreed on.

I finished my cereal and went to get dressed. When I came back, they were still arguing. "I'm going to collect eggs," I said, and Henry's eyes lit up. He stood and grabbed his jacket. As we walked out the door, he turned to Granny and said, "I'm not done arguing with you, Mrs. Fletcher. I'm going to convince you yet."

"Well, I reckon I got ten or twenty more years in me before I pass on," Granny told him. "So feel free to take your time."

First egg we found was a green one in Granny's gardening hat at the bottom of the back-porch steps. "You think I ought to change Miss Blue's name?" I asked Henry. "Since her eggs ain't so blue after all?"

"Too late for that. You'd only confuse her."

"She's laying eggs in Granny's hat instead of her nest. How's she going to get more confused than that?"

As soon as they saw us, the chickens began to cluck and squawk. That's one of the things I liked best about keeping chickens, how they fussed when I showed up, like I was some big treat they'd been waiting for all day. Reminded me of myself when my daddy actually stayed around the house on a Saturday night. I liked how I could talk to them and they'd look me right in the eye and cock their heads to one side. I felt like some genius explaining $E = mc^2$. Some days I'd talk to the chickens the whole time I was changing their water, filling up the feeder, collecting their eggs. I'd tell them about school or the stuff I'd been thinking about lately.

Made me wonder if I was turning into Henry, the way I was talking all the time. I'd been feeling kind of funny in general, like a snake shedding its skin and finding out it was a whole different animal underneath. This business of getting out and doing things, well, once you got going, it was hard to stop yourself. You start out raising chickens, you end up doing your homework half the time and even talking to a few people in your classes. You start feeling like this useful human being. It was getting so I hardly recognized myself in the mirror.

Me and Henry spent the rest of the afternoon with the chickens and Calvin, Granny's big mutt, who appeared to have left his dog buddies behind to join the flock.

"Calvin is proof," Henry told me, scrawling something into his notebook. "He's in love with these chickens. You don't fall in love with something if its brain is just a rock with some nerves." He kept writing in his notebook and muttering to himself like a mad scientist. I thought Mr. Peabody ought to give him an A just for caring so much about making his point.

That night Granny did the strangest thing she'd done so far. She tucked me into bed, like she thought I was four instead of twelve. She even patted down my hair a few times. You could say me and Granny were close, but we weren't too huggy about it. Now I was really wondering what she was up to.

"This used to be your mama's room, you know," Granny said, sitting on the edge of the bed and looking around like she hadn't sat here in a long time.

"I know, Granny. You've told me a thousand times."

Granny pointed to the wall across from the foot of the bed. "I helped her hang up that Beatles poster. Didn't have the least bit of an idea who the Beatles were, only knew they'd spelled their name wrong. Sandy said maybe that's how the English people spelled *beetle*. She was smart that way, thinking things through."

Granny leaned over and pulled the sheet up under my chin. "I've been thinking about what you said back a couple weeks ago, about you coming to live here. I ain't a good person to live with, I don't think, but maybe we could work something out. I hate to think of you stuck there with that no-good daddy of yours."

I closed my eyes. So that was Granny's other surprise, the one I'd been expecting to pop out at me from behind the couch. I let it settle over me. Now that it might happen, I couldn't hardly imagine what it would be like to move from one house to another.

"Well, you think about it, son, and let me know." Granny walked over to the door and switched off the overhead light. "You say yes, and I'll get on the phone with my lawyer first thing. Not that I have a lawyer, but I'll get me one, don't you worry."

"What do you need a lawyer for?" I asked, my eyes opening wide in the dark.

"If I'm going to get custody of you, we'll have

to go through the courts," Granny said. "And I reckon we'll have to fight your daddy pretty hard. He's too stubborn to let me get my way without making everybody miserable before it's all over."

"You want custody of me?"

"That's what you want, isn't it? I'd thought once or twice about trying to get custody way back when your mama died. But Shane and Summer was just in their early teens then, and Patrick was already a mess, always getting in trouble at school. I was afraid a judge might make me take all four kids instead of just you."

Granny stepped into the hallway and pulled the door closed behind her. I sat up in bed, smelling the smell of what used to be my mom's room. I was waiting to feel excited about Granny wanting custody of me, but every time my brain got back around to that lawyer, my stomach got hot at the center, and the burning feeling made its way up to my chest. Didn't seem right to go to court against your own father, some judge running his finger down the pages of a law book, looking for all the things your daddy was doing wrong.

I tried lying back down and thinking about camping, about how round the rocks are you find in a river, all those years of the water rushing over them and smoothing down their rough edges. I had a shelf full of river rocks at home, from the two camping trips I'd taken. Filled my backpack up with them both times, even though I knew it'd make hiking out of the woods a whole lot harder.

That's what it felt like, thinking about a lawyer going against my dad, like carrying a load of heavy rocks on my back. It wasn't the right way to go. Maybe instead me and Daddy and Granny could all sit down together and work up a schedule. Some days I'd stay at one place, some days I'd stay at the other. Daddy wasn't hardly ever home, so it ought to be all the same to him, and Granny could still go fishing in the middle of the week sometimes without worrying about having to fix me dinner.

That was such a good idea that I grinned into the darkness. For the first time in my life, I felt kind of smart. I guessed Henry and Miss Blue were rubbing off on me.

FIFTEEN

All fall me and Harrison kept racing, and all fall
I kept winning. You might not think it was a fair
match, but Harrison was the fastest kid under
the age of ten I'd ever seen. So even if I had the
advantage of being older, I still felt like he was
pretty good competition and might even beat
me one day when his legs got a little longer.

I started running on my own sometimes,
mostly through the woods behind the shiny new
neighborhoods that kept sprouting up around my
part of town like fields of mushrooms after a big
rain. I'd go after school, run from my house to
Granny's. I didn't even know what the neighborhoods were called or the names of the streets, but
I'd run every day, just about. The woods were

cool, and there was nobody around to stop me or bug me and ask me questions I didn't feel like answering. I picked out my favorite yards and trees and one or two houses I liked the looks of.

Most of the houses were all the same shape and color. But there was one right smack in the center of a new neighborhood that stood where a farm used to be. It had a screened porch, and somebody'd painted the whole thing a purple color, and it was crazy but it was pretty, too. I always liked to see that house coming into view, just because it was this wild thing in the middle of everything being the same.

The next Saturday, week after fall break, I ran all the way to Granny's to do my chicken chores. After me and Granny had that custody talk, I sort of felt like I was running home when I went to her house, even though I hadn't sat down with her and Daddy to figure things out yet. I was waiting for the right time, and I wasn't sure when that was going to be, since it was hard to imagine a time when Daddy and Granny would be happy to sit down in the same room together.

Still, I felt all light and good about my idea, and that made me faster somehow. When I reached the backyard, I found Harrison over there, checking up on the business end of my chickens, and that made me feel good too, since he was the only person I knew who liked running as much as I did. Walking up to the back porch, I could hear him and Granny discussing Miss Blue's relationship with Calvin.

"What worries me is that she's spending more time with a dog than she does with chickens," Harrison was saying. "That could have a negative impact on her laying habits. And we really need these hens to produce."

"I wouldn't worry about her egg production if I was you," Granny told him. "She lays one green egg a day, which is all you can ask for. You just got to find it." She turned and called out to me, "When you gonna build some nesting boxes, son? I found an egg in my shoe this morning."

"Was your shoe inside or outside?" I asked, coming up to the porch.

"Outside."

"Then you're lucky all you found was an egg."

Harrison gave me the once-over. "Tobin, why's your face so red?"

"Been running."

119

"Oh," he said, nodding. He turned to Granny. "He's really fast. He beats me all the time, and I'm the fastest one in my school, including all the fourth grade and all the fifth grade."

"He's always been fast," Granny commented. "He takes after me that way."

Harrison wiggled his feet, like he was ready to hit the ground running himself. "Hey, Tobin, do you think you'll try out for cross-country?"

I gave him a suspicious look. "Did Henry tell you to ask me that?"

Just that week in PE, Coach Kelly had announced we were doing a three-week unit on track and field. Soon as he said it, Henry leaned over and popped me on the arm.

"Dude, you've got to dress out for this. At least once. It's your chance to shine."

I shook my head no. I guess I wasn't feeling all that shiny right then.

"Oh, come on," Henry protested. "Think of the honor. Think of the glory." He leaned closer to me. "Think of the poetry."

"What are you talking about, son? I don't even like poetry."

Henry sighed. He leaned back against the bleacher behind him. "Where's your soul, man? Where's your sense of drama? Here we've got a chance to set the world on end. All it takes is you putting on a pair of gym shorts and running around a track. Can you imagine the looks on everyone's faces? All this time, they thought they knew everything about you, and here it turns out you're this god of speed. They don't know you at all, man."

I looked around at the kids sprawled on the bleachers listening to Coach Kelly run his mouth about proper footwear. Kids that had been looking down on me for years now on account of me being a McCauley. That sweet buzzing feeling started filling me up again as I saw myself on the track, passing each of their sorry butts one by one. I could just picture Coach Kelly with his mouth hanging open.

But what was supposed to happen after that? Was it supposed to be like a movie, where Cody Peters made an awkward walk across the track to shake my hand and say he was sorry for all the hell he'd given me? Would party invitations start piling up outside my front door? Why'd I have to prove anything to them snot buckets, anyway? They ought to be doing cartwheels and somersaults on my front yard trying to prove something to me.

"No way," I told Henry, shaking my head. "I told you, it's a waste of my time."

Henry slapped his hand on the bleacher. "Man! Why do you have to be so stubborn?" But he let it go. Wouldn't have surprised me, though, if he'd put Harrison up to dropping some hints.

"Henry didn't tell me to ask you anything," Harrison said. "I just thought if you went out for cross-country, you could put a good word in for me with the coach for when I get to middle school. Why would Henry want me to ask you about cross-country?"

"Because we're doing track in PE, and he wants me to run."

Granny eyed my feet. "Can't see how you could get much running done in them shoes, they're so floppy-looking."

"I run in 'em every day," I told her. "They work just fine."

Granny dug down into her pocket and pulled out her car keys. "Catch!" she called, throwing them in Harrison's direction. He grabbed the keys out of the air and held them out to Granny like a question.

"Go start the truck for me, son," Granny said, using the railing to pull herself up from the porch step. "We're going shopping."

"He's nine years old, Granny," I told her. "He can't start no truck."

"Then it's high time he learned how," Granny said. "I'm going to get my purse. Meet you boys out front."

"What are we going shopping for?" I called after her. She turned back toward me and grinned.

"New pair of shoes for you, of course," she said. "You got to have the right shoes for PE, especially if you're going to run."

I shook my head. Granny never bought me anything except a bag of popcorn at the movies. She must be serious about wanting me, I thought, if she's going to start laying out money for clothes. I was smiling when I got in the truck. I have to say, it felt good to be wanted, son. Felt real good.

SIXTEEN

I let Granny buy me some new shoes, smoke-gray ones with black stripes. Harrison took a look at the brand name and said they were good ones, like real runners wore. They felt good on my feet, that was for sure. First time I took a run through the woods with those shoes on, I felt like a streak of lightning, son, the way I zipped over all the leaves and broken branches in my path.

But just because I had new shoes didn't mean I was going to run in PE. I knew it wouldn't change anything, no matter what Henry said. Besides, them shoes didn't make my legs look any less scrawny. Why get everybody looking at me again? Things were better than they'd been in a long time. I had a friend and I hadn't even been looking for one, I was doing okay in a couple of my classes, I even had an extra-credit project. As far as school was concerned, I wanted everything to stay just like it was.

What I didn't know was things at home were about to blow sky-high.

It all started ordinary enough. I was over at Granny's, holding up one of Miss Blue's green eggs to the sun. It was like one of them Easter eggs we'd made when we were little, when I still believed in the Easter bunny.

Granny came down from the house, shaking feathers out of her gardening hat. "Your chickens are taking over everything," she said. "Just look at that one over there, sweet-talking my dog." Granny pointed over to where Miss Blue and Calvin were walking along where the ferns grew at the edge of the woods. "Can't keep them two apart, and Calvin likes to sleep indoors come winter. I'm gonna have chicken feathers in my bed."

She jammed the hat onto her head. "Anyway, what I come down to tell you is your feathers-for-brains brother Shane is on his way over. Bringing me a carburetor, he claims."

"Why would he do that for?"

"Says he's cleaning out that backyard over there. Your daddy's orders."

Five minutes later, Shane pulled up in Granny's driveway. "Hey, old woman!" he yelled when he saw Granny. "Why ain't you out fishing, anyway, nice day like this?"

"I've been tethered to this house by five chickens, seven dogs, and three loads of laundry stinking up the kitchen. That Talmadge Lumberton dropped off his work clothes, asking me to do him the favor. His machine's on the fritz."

Shane saw me and winked. "Sounds like Granny's got a new boyfriend. Maybe this one'll stick."

When Shane was done hauling out the carburetor and dumping it on Granny's carport, where it would probably sit for three years until Granny got around to doing something with it, he threw my bike into his truck and gave me a ride home.

"How come Daddy's got you cleaning up the

yard?" I asked him, rolling down the window to let the wind blow in my face.

Shane pulled out onto the main road. "Don't know, but he's mad as hell about something, I can tell you that much."

When we got home, I helped Shane haul stuff to the driveway. "My buddy Teddy from work ought to be here in about fifteen minutes to collect all this mess," he said.

"Why do you got so much of everything?" I asked after a couple of trips to and from the backyard. Even with all my running, I was starting to feel out of wind from carrying that junk. "You planning to build yourself a whole fleet of cars?"

"Nope, just one perfect automobile." Shane got the same lovey-dovey look on his face he got when he talked about Becca. "It was like I was trying to put a puzzle together. Every time I was near a junkyard or a used auto supplies place, I had to go in and see if I could find one of the pieces I was looking for. Well, I found a bunch of pieces, all right, but never ones that fit together in exactly the right way."

I dumped a jumble of parts by a tower of tires. "Maybe one day you'll get rich and you can buy yourself the perfect car."

Shane shook his head. "Wouldn't be the same as putting it together myself."

The backyard was starting to clear out. It surprised me to see how much space there was. It'd been clogged up so long with all Shane's carburetors and radiators, engine blocks and coils and coils of black hoses snaking this way and that, that I'd forgotten there was room to move back there. You could have a whole flock of chickens if you wanted.

A horn honked out front and Shane's friend Teddy, who was about as tall and wide as a deluxe refrigerator, hopped out of his truck. We spent the next twenty minutes putting the first load onto the truck. It was going to take at least three loads to get everything gone.

I was handing up a steering wheel to Teddy when my dad pulled up behind Teddy's truck. It was only four o'clock in the afternoon, way too early for him to be back from Uncle Rob's. It made my stomach all nervous to see him home at the wrong time. It brought back the memory of when my mom was sick and Daddy was either at the hospital or wandering around the house all afternoon like a ghost.

"What you doing standing there with your mouth open?" Daddy called, getting out of the car. "Can't you see I need some help?"

SEVENTEEN

Daddy pulled two Food Lion bags out of the trunk of his car. I grabbed them from him, and he followed me into the house carrying four more.

"Man, it stinks in here, did you ever notice that?" Daddy dumped his bags on the floor by the kitchen and looked around. "Patrick, is that you? You wash your socks lately?"

Patrick was sitting in front of the TV. "It ain't me. Just nobody's taken out the trash in days, is all."

"Well, nobody's stopping you," Daddy told him. "Why don't you get your behind off that couch and get that stink out of here?"

Patrick stared at the screen like he wasn't

going nowhere, but then he must have changed his mind about that being a good idea. He pushed himself off of the couch as slow as a person could while still actually moving.

Daddy turned toward the kitchen and looked around for a minute. Then he rubbed my shoulder. "Well, son, I reckon it's time we took care of this. Company's coming, and the house has got to look nice."

I tried to think of who might be coming to see us, but nobody came to mind. We weren't the kind of family that made people feel welcome. "Who is it?"

"Social workers, first thing Tuesday morning," Daddy said. "Turns out your granny don't think much of my child-rearing methods, so she's called up the Department of Social Services and told them to come check out our situation. Rumor has it that you're a neglected child." His voice made it sound like he thought it was funny, but his face told a different story.

I took a few steps backwards and flopped down on the couch. My stomach went cold and my face went hot. What could be going on in

Granny's head? "I didn't tell her to do that," I said.

Daddy gave me a strange look. "I didn't say that you did."

I shook my head. Granny was supposed to wait to hear from me what I wanted her to do, but I hadn't told her yet. Now she'd gone and pulled a stunt that was a hundred times worse than driving up on the middle-school sidewalk.

Now I didn't have any choice but do whatever I could to help Daddy make this house fit for me to live in. But after the social workers had come and gone and given Daddy a good report, there'd be no way he'd let me stay parttime over at Granny's. Couldn't say I blamed him, either. It's one thing to hate somebody. It's a whole other thing to get Social Services on their butt.

Daddy walked toward the kitchen, carrying the grocery bags. "I aim to cook us some dinner, but we're going to have to clear this mess up and out first."

My arms and legs were aching from helping Shane clear out the backyard, but I could feel the push in me to make things right in the house. Since I was already an old hand at dish-washing, I started at the sink. Daddy opened up a cabinet. "Sandy had a system for all this stuff," he said, pointing to the few cans up on the shelves. "But I don't know what it was. Salt on the top, soup on the bottom? You think it makes a difference?"

"She always kept the sweet stuff on the top shelf, so me and Patrick wouldn't eat it," I said, all the sudden remembering. "Like them choco-late kisses she used to get. Only, me and Patrick would climb up on the counter and find 'em anyway."

Daddy nodded. "Kept her cigarettes up there, too, because she figured Shane'd be too lazy to climb up after them. 'Course, he got so tall he could just reach up and get 'em once he was twelve." He turned to look at me. "You smoke?"

"Nah." I could have said, "Your mom dies of cancer, you don't smoke cigarettes," but I kept my mouth shut.

"Good. I never did either. It's a stupid habit."

"I don't smoke," Patrick said, hauling in

the trash can. "Tried it once, but it made me throw up."

Daddy popped him on the back. "There may be hope for you yet, son."

Patrick scowled, but you could tell he liked the idea of someone feeling hopeful about him. "Can I go back and watch TV now?"

Daddy nodded. He turned his attention back to the cabinet. "Okay then, salt on the bottom, sugar on top, and soup in the middle." He took out the motley crew of cans on the shelves and put them back up according to his plan. Then he pulled some more cans out of the Food Lion bags. "Got us some soup and baked beans. People always like soup and baked beans."

"Got 'em for what?" I asked, scrubbing on a cereal bowl with cornflakes crusted around the rim.

"I got them to have," Daddy said. "To eat when you get hungry."

"Like supplies?"

"Yeah, like supplies. Don't people usually keep food in the house?"

Not us, I almost said, but I just nodded instead.

"I got the large-size, maple-flavored baked beans, that's the best." Daddy sounded all proud, putting up the tall cans. "They go on the soup shelf."

Daddy commented upon every item he put away. Baked beans, pinto beans, bag of white rice, sugar for coffee, chicken with noodle soup, tomato soup, cream of mushroom soup (which he was pretty sure you could use if you wanted to make a casserole), salt, pepper, onion powder, chili powder, spaghetti sauce, and canned mushrooms to doctor up the spaghetti sauce with. Two one-pound boxes of spaghetti, two taco dinner mixes, and three Hamburger Helpers.

Next, he turned to the refrigerator. "Hand me a garbage bag from that sack on the table, would you? I'm just throwing everything in here away. It all stinks like fish and rotten something. I can't even tell what half of this junk is."

Five minutes later Daddy was kneeling in front of the fridge with a bucket of hot water beside him and a sponge in his hand. I'd worked my way through the dishes and started scrubbing down the stove. I opened up the oven door to find three ancient pieces of pizza curling up at me. I didn't even want to think about how long they'd been in there.

Once me and Daddy got going, we couldn't make ourselves stop. We finished up in the kitchen and headed out into the living room, each of us carrying a trash bag to collect pizza boxes and soda cans and the bits and pieces of junk that collect around the corners of a place, rubber bands and used-up napkins and gum wrappers and little pieces of potato chips.

"It's getting there," Daddy said, stuffing a Subway wrapper into his bag and looking around the room. "But something's missing. It looks clean, but it don't smell clean, the way it did when Sandy was done picking up."

"Furniture polish." Patrick turned up his nose and made a sniffy sound. "Lemon-flavored furniture polish."

"We got any of that?"

"Dried up by now, if we do," I told him.

"We'll get us some tomorrow, then. Let's get this trash outside and start cooking dinner."

When Daddy chopped the onions to throw

136

in with the hamburger for our Hamburger Helper dinner, his eyes filled up with tears. I handed him a wad of napkins from the brand-new pack on the kitchen table. He blew his nose into one and started to laugh. "Man, I was feeling all right two minutes ago."

Patrick stuck his head in the kitchen doorway. "What happened, Daddy? Tobin start singing and it made you cry?"

Daddy laughed some more. "You remember how he used to play the kazoo when he was a baby? Singing them baby noises in that little plastic kazoo? Your mama thought he was a genius, figuring that out."

"She didn't think he was a genius that time he took all the knives out of the drawer to play pirate with."

Daddy turned and gave Patrick a questioning look. "I thought it was you who was all the time playing pirate."

"Maybe it was, maybe it wasn't," Patrick said. "Talk to my lawyer about it."

"I'll do that." Daddy went back to chopping onions. "You hungry, Pat?"

Patrick pulled out a chair and sat down across the table from me. I waited for him to say something snotty that would ruin the good mood. Instead he said, "That smells good, what you're cooking, Daddy."

I couldn't believe Patrick had passed up a chance to make a smart-aleck remark. It was like a regular family, the way all of us were sitting here, dinner cooking on the stove. I forgot all about the social workers we were getting ready to impress.

Daddy whistled the theme song from the 10 o'clock news. The smell of the onions frying in the pan filled the room. Patrick tapped his fingers against the table and hummed.

I started tapping my fingers in rhythm with Patrick's, thinking as hard as I could how I could keep up this good mood we were all sharing. I'd compliment Daddy on his cooking, I decided, and I'd do the dishes after dinner. Then I'd do my homework, even though it was Saturday night. Might even ask Daddy for help on the math.

I looked down the road to the future. I'd do

my homework every night after dinner, and I'd do my weekend homework on Friday nights. I couldn't do one super-big thing at school, like become class president or make the honor roll before Christmas, but I knew a little thing I could do. I could run in PE. I could win a race, then come home and tell Daddy all about it. He'd be so excited, he might even turn off the TV when I told him how I was faster than the speed of light.

EIGHTEEN

"You have got the chicken legs, my man, there can be no argument about that."

Henry whacked my left knee with one of his gym socks. "How can you run all the time and still be so scrawny?"

I gave him my evil eye. "You want me to run today or not?"

Henry held up his hands. "Did I say there was anything wrong with having scrawny legs? Did you catch a note of judgment in my voice? I don't think so."

The Legion Middle School gym shorts felt scratchy on my legs. The fabric was something fake that you wouldn't want to hold a match too close to. Cotton T-shirt with a stupid cougar jumping across it. There wasn't a cougar within three hundred miles of this place, so why'd they go naming the school mascot after one?

"Nice shoes, McCauley," some kid called out from the other side of the locker room. "You rob a shoe store over the weekend?"

"Ignore him," Henry told me, lacing up his sneakers. He wore white Chucks, the opposite of his black Chucks he wore the rest of the day.

"Didn't hear nothing but the wind," I said, trying to sound cool. I didn't feel too cool, though. I was ready to run, ready to get it over with so I could go back to not dressing out for gym.

Everybody filed from the locker room through a door that led to the outside, taking a path past the tennis courts and down to the track. All the smart-aleck remarks being made about me bounced off my buzzing arms and legs and sped into the universe.

Coach Kelly was waiting for us on the track, clipboard in his hand. He looked us over, checked our names on the roll. When his eyes landed on me, he didn't say nothing, he just stared an extra second.

"Fifty-yard dash today, guys," he called out. "Two at a time. Line up, two lines, and let's get moving."

I got in line behind Henry and eyeballed the guys in the other line, trying to figure who I'd get matched up with. I was counting down the row when Coach Kelly's hand yanked me over to the grass.

"Uh-uh, McCauley, no way. You don't dress out for two months, and today you decide you've come to play? What is it? You only participate in the stuff that interests you? Yeah, I know guys like you. Well, you can rest yourself on the bleachers over there for a couple of days. I'll let you know when you can join in our reindeer games."

He pushed me toward the stands. Henry broke out of line and followed me over. "That is a man seriously in need of some chicken time, to chill his bones out," he said as we sat down. "How they let someone like him be an authority figure is beyond me."

Just then Coach Kelly blew his whistle and Cody Peters and Ralph Jacobs took off. Ralph had a pretty good stride, nice and long, no wasted effort, but Cody was just plain fast. He didn't even bother to turn around when he crossed the finish line to make sure he'd won. He didn't have to.

"So why don't you run anyway?" Henry said after two more pairs of legs had pounded down the track. "There's eight lanes on that track, and they're only using two. You could just go up there and start running when the whistle blows. What's Coach Kelly going to do? Tackle you?"

"I can't do that," I said, even though I couldn't think of one good reason why not. I had to remind myself of why I was racing. I wanted a good story I could tell my dad when he got home from work that night, something that would make him proud.

"Every day the world needs a little shaking up, my man," Henry said, standing. "And you're just the dude to do it. You're Chicken Boy, Fastest Kid in the West. Don't let the Man get in your way."

"What a bunch of fart blowers," I muttered, getting up and standing next to Henry. My guts were jumping and my knees were knocking, but I started walking anyway.

Russell Pearson and Jamie Whitesall were lined up to run. Coach Kelly was checking off something on his clipboard, so he didn't even see me as I took my place in the second-to-outside lane. Don't know why, but none of them nose pickers said a word as I squatted down in the starting position, hands on the track, one knee bent, one leg stretched behind me, and waited for the whistle.

"McCauley!" Coach Kelly's voice screamed after me two seconds after his whistle blew, but his words couldn't catch me. I was out of town, son, good as gold, running like no tomorrow. Fifty yards ain't nothing, takes you ten seconds or less, less if you're me, and I was over that line in no time flat with nothing but empty space behind me.

I slowed down to a trot, passing the guys who'd already run, sprawled out in the grass by the finish line. None of them said a word. Them sapsuckers just stared like a ghost had arrived in their midst. Even Cody Peters kept his mouth shut for once in his life.

You can bet your sweet butt that Henry didn't.

"No man is an island!" I could hear him yelling as he ran up the track toward me. "NO man is an island, do you hear me? Every man is a piece of the continent, a part of the main!"

He held my hand into the air for victory and turned to the crowd on the grass. "May I introduce you to Tobin McCauley, fastest kid in this school, in this country, probably in this hemisphere. I hear anyone treat him with anything but respect ever again and I will shed my peaceable ways and have your butt on a platter. Any questions?"

Cody Peters opened his mouth. "Ain't got none," he said in a slow, retarded-sounding voice. Henry started toward him, but I put my arm out to hold him back.

"This ain't your fight," I told him. Henry nodded and took a step back. I turned to Cody. "You want to race, Cody? Fifty yards, nothing to put a strain on you."

I waited for some smart talk. I waited for Cody Peters to swagger over and push me in the chest. I waited for him to take off running, to try to get a head start.

Instead, he just shook his head. "Nah, I'm not in the mood. Besides, I'd hate to wreck your lucky streak."

I smiled. I grinned a grin a mile wide. I knew something, and everybody else sitting there knew it too. Cody Peters was afraid.

And he wasn't afraid of winning.

NINETEEN

You wouldn't believe how cocky I was when I talked to them social workers, son. I was Chicken Boy, the Fastest Kid in the West, and I wasn't doing one thing I didn't want to do. I played it right down the middle, said I loved Granny and I knew she was trying to do what she thought was right, but my home was with my dad.

The tall, pencil-thin social worker, named Ms. Brighton, smiled at me from across the kitchen table. She had a gap the size of the Grand Canyon between her two front teeth. "When your grandmother filed a report with us, she said there was rarely food in the house for you to eat. Is that true, Tobin?" She twirled her pen in her fingers like it was a baton, waiting for me to answer.

I chewed on my top lip with my bottom teeth, stalling. Didn't want to make Granny out for a liar, but I didn't want to tell the truth, either. I needed to cover my dad's back so they couldn't say he wasn't doing a good job. Finally I pointed to the cabinets over the kitchen counter. "Take a look for yourself," I said. "There was plenty of food last time I checked."

Mrs. Townsend, the other social worker, who looked too young to be a Mrs., tried to pierce me with her squinty black eyes. "But what is the general trend? Is there usually food in the house? Have you always felt like you had enough to eat?"

I looked out the window over the sink. I could see the gas station next door, could see a man cleaning his windshield with a handful of Kleenex. He'd spit on the glass, then rub the Kleenex around. It looked to me like he was making the windshield dirtier, but maybe I had a bad angle on the situation.

"Tobin?" Ms. Brighton asked brightly. Everything about her was bright, her name, her voice, her pink sweater with a rose made out of dark pink beads smack in the middle of her chest. "We need to know the answers to these questions so we can make an informed recommendation as to your future care."

"I already told you, there's plenty of food."

Mrs. Townsend sighed. It wasn't one of those nice Miss Thesman sighs, full of sad feelings and good intentions. It was a sigh that said, *Young man, you are getting on my nerves.* I grinned. Mrs. Townsend was the sort of bean snorter whose nerves you wanted to get on. She looked like a teenager who'd raided her mom's closet for Career Day. She was the last person in the world I'd let boss me around, son.

Ms. Brighton tapped her pen against her clipboard a few times. "Moving on," she said, still trying to sound cheerful. "How much time a week would you say your father spends with you?"

"Plenty," I said, leaning back in my chair.

"And how would you define 'plenty'?" Ms.

Brighton asked. I'll say this for her, she didn't give up easy.

"I'd define it as being enough."

"An hour a day?"

"More or less."

Ms. Brighton wrote something on her paper. She was still smiling, but the smile was pulled thin across her lips. "Your grandmother said you had the flu last winter, and your father refused to take you to the doctor so she had to do it. Is this true?"

"He couldn't get off work," I said flatly. "That ain't refusing to do it."

"She said she hadn't heard from you in several days so she stopped by, and you had a 104-degree temperature. You were alone in the house and delirious."

"I had a bad cold is all," I said, even though I could remember the fever buzzing through my dreams, turning me hot one second, freezing the next. "Granny's exaggerating."

I figured as long as I said everything was okay, sooner or later they'd let the matter drop. The house was clean, my fingernails were clean, and thanks to me and Shane, the backyard was clean. At that very second, my upstanding daddy was out front raking leaves. Open the fridge and you'd find enough food to feed a family for a month. What else could these sapsuckers care about? I knew I had this situation under control, son. A couple of half-baked social workers couldn't touch me.

"What'd you call up Social Services for?" I hissed at Granny on the phone that night, careful not to let anyone hear who I was talking to. "I had a plan worked out for me coming to stay with you, and now you're jumping five miles in the wrong direction."

"You're the one who said you wanted to live with me," Granny said. "So now I finally agree with you, and you're giving me a hard time?"

That was on a Tuesday. On Thursday morning, I was sitting on the couch, shoving stuff into my backpack, when I looked out of the living-room window and saw a black Nissan Sentra pull up into the driveway. Ms. Brighton stepped out. A police car pulled in behind her.

Patrick opened the front door. When he saw the police officer, he said, "If you're gonna search my room, you better have a warrant."

The cop grinned and pulled out a sheet of white paper folded like a brochure. "Consider yourself served, kid."

Ms. Brighton gave the cop a sharp look. "We're here to see Tobin. Is he home?"

I came to the door carrying my backpack. Granny was supposed to pick me up in five minutes. "How come you're back?" I asked Ms. Brighton. "Did you forget to ask me some questions?"

Ms. Brighton smiled at me, only this time her smile wasn't so bright. "Tobin, we feel this is not the best environment for you at this time. Now, further assessments will have to be made, and a judge will make the final decision, but for now we feel you should be in what we call a neutral zone. Is your father home?"

I shook my head no. Ms. Brighton turned to the cop and nodded her head. He relaxed his shoulders some, like this wasn't going to be such a hard job after all. Then she turned back to me. "Your father will be informed at his place of employment later this morning. You'll be able to see him tomorrow."

It was like all her talk was running into my left ear and squirting out through my right. Was she taking me to Granny's house? I nodded toward the officer. "What's he doing here?"

"Sometimes these situations can be, well, difficult." Ms. Brighton sniffed, then turned the wattage back up on her toothy grin. "We'll take you to the house where you'll be staying in the meantime. Your school has been notified that you won't be present today."

"What about me?" Patrick asked from the couch. "You gonna take me somewhere? How about someplace where they got a satellite dish? Cable sucks."

"Your case is being investigated separately," Ms. Brighton told him. "For now, Officer Fowley will be happy to escort you to school."

Patrick picked up the remote control and aimed it at the TV. "First period don't start till eight forty-five. We got plenty of time."

Ms. Brighton stood at my bedroom door as I

threw some clothes into a suitcase she'd lugged in from the trunk of her car. "Does my dad know what you're doing?" I asked her, grabbing some socks from my drawer.

"He's aware that this was a possibility."

"You taking me to my granny's? She got custody of me now?"

Ms. Brighton shook her head, then checked her watch. "No, you'll be placed in a temporary foster-care situation. Now, be sure to get your toothbrush and whatever other toiletries you might need. We should be going."

Soon as I got in Ms. Brighton's car, I felt itchy, and that itchiness spread through me until it felt like I had ants under my skin. It wasn't until Ms. Brighton asked me to please quit knocking my head against the window that I realized it wasn't an itch and it wasn't ants, it was the feeling that if I saw my granny on the side of the road, I'd jump out of the car and fly into her face, every stinking, charbroiled cussword I could think of coming out of my mouth. She'd messed up my entire life with one dirtball report to Social Services, and now there wasn't nothing anybody could do about it.

"Tobin, I think you'll like the Paulsens, the family who will be caring for you," Ms. Brighton said, clicking on the radio. Some syrupy music spilled out of the speakers. Made me want to jump through the roof.

"I don't like nobody," I told her. "Especially not strangers." I gave her a hard look so she'd get my point.

"A stranger's just a friend you haven't met yet," Ms. Brighton chirped. She flashed me one of her famous smiles. "This is all going to work out, Tobin, you'll see." Then she started humming along with the scrambled gut-puke song playing on the radio.

I banged my head on the window a couple more times. Them ants kept marching under my skin. Red ants. Fire ants. Ants that didn't want to do nothing but burn down the world.

TWENTY

The house Ms. Brighton took me to sat back on a hill overlooking a wide street lined with houses that all looked pretty much the same, beige or gray, blank-faced as the rain. I'd finally made it to the shiny suburbs. I turned my head back and forth, two, three, four times, looking for a way out.

A woman around Granny's age, maybe a little younger, opened the door before we even got up the front steps. She looked like somebody's grandmother in a long-distance commercial, soft white sweater and blue pants, rich but nice, like she'd give you good presents at Christmas. "Tobin," she said, like we'd known each other for years. "This must be a strange day for you. Please come in."

Her name was Peggy Paulsen. When she asked if I'd rather call her Peggy or Mrs. Paulsen, I told her that Mrs. Paulsen was fine by me. That made her smile. "You have nice manners, don't you? That's quite an exceptional thing in a boy your age."

After Ms. Brighton left, Mrs. Paulsen sat me down at her dining-room table and gave me a glass of milk and a big wedge of chocolate pound cake. Then she showed me where the wide-screen TV was. Every couple of hours she brought me food of some kind or another, a bowl of grapes, a tuna sandwich, a napkin filled with Oreo cookies. I was careful not to get crumbs all over her tweedy couch.

Between all the food and the TV, I felt half asleep all day. At some point I wondered if I was allowed to make any phone calls, and I wondered who I'd call if I could. It was like my brain wouldn't quite click all the way on.

Partway through a rerun of *The Simpsons*, I heard a key turn in the front door. Footsteps shuffled in the hallway and stopped, another door opened and closed, and then Mrs. Paulsen and a white-haired man came into the TV room.

"Tobin, I'd like you to meet my husband. He is a professor of anthropology at the university." Mrs. Paulsen pushed the man a few feet forward. He tugged on his bow tie and ran a hand through his hair, which flopped over his forehead like a white comma.

"Hello, Tobin," he said, coughing a little. "We're very glad you're here. Well, perhaps *glad* isn't the right word, as we'd rather you be in your own home under happy circumstances. But you're not, you're here. And you are very welcome in our home."

After he was done, he gave me a little bow from the waist, like I was a visiting king or the president. I nodded my head back at him, royal-like, and said, "Thanks."

Mr. Paulsen bowed again. "I shall wash up for dinner, then. Mrs. Paulsen tells me we're having meat loaf, a personal favorite of mine, and of yours as well, I hope."

A few seconds later, I heard him pad up the

stairs. Mrs. Paulsen smiled at me. "He was very happy to hear you'd be with us for a few days. Our children are grown and gone. It's so nice to have a young person in the house."

"So, Tobin," Mr. Paulsen said after we'd passed around a platter of sliced meat loaf, bowls of peas and mashed potatoes, and a basket of yeast rolls, "what is it that you enjoy doing most when you're not in school?"

I couldn't think of anything. I couldn't even think of where I lived or where I went to school. It was like I'd been shot out of a cannon into space and had landed on an alien planet where I didn't speak the language and could barely breathe the air.

Mr. and Mrs. Paulsen smiled at me expectantly, like they thought some great answer was about to come tumbling out of my mouth. Finally, I remembered something from my former life. "I raise chickens with my friend Henry."

This answer seemed to make Mr. and Mrs. Paulsen the happiest people on the planet, whichever planet it was that we happened to be on.

"Chickens!" Mr. Paulsen exclaimed, slapping the edge of the table. "I raised chickens myself as a boy. Tried to get my sons interested, but they had sports on the brain and couldn't be bothered."

"We've thought about building a coop in the backyard," Mrs. Paulsen added. "But we feel almost certain that the neighborhood covenant wouldn't permit it."

"What's that?" I spooned another mound of potatoes on my plate. All the sudden I was starving. Knowing the Paulsens liked chickens as much as I did made me feel a little better about my situation. How bad could they be? They'd probably like Henry, too, if they ever met him.

Mrs. Paulsen reached over and dropped two more rolls beside my plate. "Just the rules that all the homeowners in this subdivision have to follow. What colors you're allowed to paint your house, what sort of yard decorations you can put out, that sort of thing."

"Chickens would brighten up this neighborhood a lot," I said through a mouthful of meat loaf. "Give it a little personality."

"I agree, one hundred percent!" Mr. Paulsen said, laughing. He dished out some more meat loaf and plopped it down next to my mashed potatoes. "Mrs. Paulsen and I have often wondered if we ought to move to some place a bit more festive. It does seem a shame to grow old in a neighborhood where they don't allow chickens."

"We've considered moving to one of the coastal towns when Mr. Paulsen retires," Mrs. Paulsen added. "We could buy a house and paint it pink if we wanted. A nice coral pink."

"And raise chickens," Mr. Paulsen said, nodding his head. You could tell the idea was planting itself in his brain. He looked at me and smiled. "Chickens! What an interesting young man."

Mrs. Paulsen served me another hunk of chocolate pound cake for dessert. She and Mr. Paulsen drank coffee, smiling at me over the edges of their cups. After I'd taken my last bite of cake, I suddenly felt so tired I wanted to curl up under the dining-room table and sleep for weeks.

"This boy needs to go to bed," Mr. Paulsen reported to Mrs. Paulsen. "I'll go get a glass of milk to put on his bedside table."

As soon as the light clicked off, my brain came wide awake. I blinked hard into the darkness, trying to picture in my head the trail that led from my house to the Paulsens', the paperwork that must have been filed, the phone calls from this person to that one. Somewhere, somehow, somebody made a mistake. A mistake as big as the moon. I rolled from one side of the bed to the other, the blankets twisting up into a rope. It felt like hours until I fell asleep and only minutes before I woke up to the sun shining in through my window.

"Do you like a hot breakfast or a cold breakfast, Tobin?" Mrs. Paulsen called out when she heard my footsteps on the stairs the next morning. "And what kind of juice do you prefer? We have orange, cranberry, and grapefruit."

I was just about to tell her that I drank Coke for breakfast, when the sound of an engine puttering at the curb got my attention. It wasn't the putter of a high-end motor. Granny. I could just picture her sky blue 1984 Toyota truck parked in the driveway, her navy blue sneaker tapping impatiently on the accelerator. I sat on the bottom step for a second, wanting to go back to sleep, I felt so relaxed all the sudden. Granny was here. We'd drive over to the Social Services office together, I figured, and she'd take back that report she filed, apologizing left and right.

I stood up and pressed my face against the little glass panel by the front door. Two houses down my dad's old rusty Chrysler sat parked by the mailbox, exhaust fanning from the tailpipe. I looked up and down the street, sure that Granny's truck would be there, too. It wasn't.

Without bothering to tell Mrs. Paulsen where I was going, I grabbed my jacket off the staircase and rushed out the front door. Daddy pushed the passenger-side door open soon as he saw me running to his car. "Get in here, son," he called. "I don't got all day."

TWENTY-ONE

I threw my jacket in the backseat and climbed in next to Daddy. "You kidnapping me?"

My dad shook his head in disgust. "You can't kidnap your own child, no matter what them pissant social workers say. But we ain't going anywhere. It's against the rules for me to be here in the first place."

"Then why'd you come?"

Daddy tapped his fingers along the top of the steering wheel. "Just wanted to see how you were doing. Them people they got you with, are they treating you okay?"

I nodded. "They're nice. They like chickens."

Daddy grinned. "Is that what it takes to get your seal of approval these days?"

"Don't know," I said, stretching out my legs.

Daddy reached over and rubbed my shoulder. "I'm sorry about this mess, son. It's probably all my fault. Your granny called me again a few weeks ago about your mom's clothes. I told her to give it up because them clothes were staying put. Called her a few names, told her to get a life. Now I'm wondering if this ain't her way of getting back at me. Trying to get custody of my son over a couple of shirts."

My skin went lizard cold. "You think she'd do that? You think since she can't get some shirts, she's gonna try to get me instead?"

"She might," Daddy said. Then he looked at me and tried to take it back. "Aw, she's just a crazy old lady, Tobin. I don't even mean that in a bad way. You can't take it too personally. She ain't been right since your mama died."

I pulled on the door handle. "I need to go to school," I said. "I need to eat breakfast. They got three kinds of juice." I felt like a robot talking. Day before I'd been mad as a bear on a bad morning. Now you could have stuck pins in my arms and I wouldn't have noticed. I guess my system got overloaded on junk to be mad about, and it all the sudden shut down like somebody pulled the plug.

"Tobin," Daddy called after me as I started walking back to the Paulsens' house, but I just kept going, one robot foot after the other. Mrs. Paulsen was waiting for me at the door. "The bus will be here in ten minutes, dear," she said, taking my arm and guiding me down the hallway to the kitchen. "You need to eat up. Your lunch is in that bag on the table. I have a few lunch boxes in the pantry, but surely a boy your age doesn't carry a lunch box. Or are things different now?"

"Paper bag's fine," I said. "It don't matter."

Here's the first thing I learned that morning: You eat a big breakfast, a bus won't make you feel so sick. Your stomach's just got to have a little in it to make the ride go smooth.

The second thing I learned is that school ain't a half-bad place to be sometimes. Say your granny turns on you, and the social workers get ahold of you, and there ain't a thing your daddy can do, and all your brother cares about is living someplace with a satellite dish. Say you find yourself living on a street you never set eyes on before, sleeping in a room that's not yours, a room that smells good but it don't smell right. Son, you will be happier than Christmas when your school comes into view, take my word for it.

I found Henry at his locker talking to Daniel Stottlemeyer. Daniel was this kid who'd adopted us at lunchtime. One day he just showed up at our table, sat down at the far corner, and started eating his lunch off the yellow cafeteria tray. Me and Henry looked at each other like, *What's he doing here?* and then Henry said, real loud, "Hey, Dan, what's the plan? How's everything shakin'?" which about cracked me up because Daniel Stottlemeyer ain't an everything-shakin' kinda guy.

"It's Daniel," the kid said. He had them inch-thick glasses that geeky kids on TV wear but you almost never see in real life. "No one calls me Dan."

"So, what's the haps in the lion's den, young

Daniel?" Henry spit out a sunflower seed into his hand and flicked it into his little tofu container.

Daniel Stottlemeyer shrugged. "I've got a test in pre-algebra. It's going to be hard, but I think I'll do well. I've been studying."

And then he got down to the eating part of things and stayed quiet the rest of the time. Next day, there he was again. Day after that Ryan Koestler sat down across from Daniel Stottlemeyer and plopped a brown paper bag and three cartons of chocolate milk on the table. He pulled a peanut-butter sandwich out of the bag, popped open a milk, and ate him some lunch. I knew Ryan from sixth grade, but I couldn't think of one thing about him except that his mom had brought cupcakes to school on his last birthday. Seemed kinda babyish, sixth-grade birthday cupcakes, but I ate one or two, just to be polite about it.

The day after fat Farley Overstreet took a seat and started tearing into a plate of cheeseburgers like he hadn't seen a square meal in months, Henry showed up with a checkerboard. He ate his lunch, then set up the game. Daniel made some remark about how he preferred chess, but the fact is everybody likes a game of checkers, even if they're too snotty to admit it. Pretty soon we had us a tournament going, and Ryan was keeping track of who played who next on the back of his math notebook.

Now, seeing Henry and Daniel talking, I felt like King Normal Person, just walking down the hall to my buddy's locker. When Henry saw me, he called out, "Dude, I got some news you're not going to like."

"Lay it on me, son," I said, thinking that when it came to giving bad news, Henry wasn't nothing but an amateur.

"Peabody says we both have to give oral presentations on the chicken project if we're going to get credit for it."

I dropped my backpack to the floor and leaned back against the row of lockers. "I ain't doing an oral presentation. Don't need extra credit anyway. I got a C+ average in that class."

"But if you don't, I won't get credit, either," Henry said. "It's gotta be you and me both, or nada. You report what you've observed directly, I report what I've observed, together it comes together into one big scientific panorama. Peabody wants the big picture, dude, and that takes two."

"Peabody is a stickler for oral presentations," Daniel added. "He won't change his mind about this."

I started laughing so hard I was almost crying. I felt a little crazy right then, the normalness of school and worrying about grades mixed up with the rest of my life, which was anything but normal.

When I finally caught my breath to talk, I said, "All right, I'll give a report. Just tell me what to say."

Henry thwacked me on the back. "Dude, you'll think of something."

By lunchtime I'd gotten sort of evened out, not numb, but not laughing and crying my head off, either. Maricruz Garza came and sat next to me while I played checkers against Ryan, and when I won, she asked if she could play me next. "I'm the checkers champion of my family," she said, moving to the seat across the table from me. "Nobody beats me."

By the time our kings were chasing each other around the board, we had a crowd. Most of them were cheering for Maricruz, but not like they hated me or anything. When I finally won, Maricruz reached over to shake my hand and said, "Good game, Tobin," and some other kid said, "It was luck, nothing but luck." It's hard to explain, but I felt like a regular person right then, someone people could tease and it didn't mean nothing.

For the first time in my life, I didn't want school to end. I knew who I was in school and how I felt about things. My feet were dragging as I walked down the corridor to the bus. I might've turned around and looked for a janitor's closet to hide in over the weekend, except my stomach started growling. The Paulsens were pretty nice people, I reminded myself, and they weren't stingy when it came to laying the food on the table.

The thought of food got my feet moving faster in the direction of the bus. I could almost taste that chocolate pound cake. A little cake, a glass of milk, some wide-screen TV watching. I

was working myself up for an afternoon of serious couch time when I heard my name called over the top of the crowd.

Granny was parked in the vice principal's spot, her window rolled down. "I came to give you a ride," she yelled. "I don't think that's against the rules and don't much care if it is."

I didn't bother answering. Just found bus 348 and hopped on. I took a seat where I couldn't see Granny's truck outside the window, closing my eyes just to make extra sure I wouldn't have to look at her face again. The driver put the bus into gear, and I turned my thoughts back to pound cake. I wondered what Mrs. Paulsen was making for dinner that night. When I opened my eyes again, the bus was pulling out into the road. As far as I was concerned, my granny wasn't nothing but a thing of the past.

TWENTY-TWO

On Saturday Mr. Paulsen showed me how to make a nesting box. He remembered how to do it pretty well from his boyhood days. Didn't take but thirty minutes to nail that sucker together, and afterward we sat in Mr. Paulsen's garage and admired our work. Only thing missing was a chicken to put in it.

"You take this to your room," Mr. Paulsen said, handing the box to me like a gift. "It might be nice to have a box in which to store special things. A box that belongs to you and nobody else."

"We could sneak us some chickens into the garage," I pointed out. "There's got to be a way around them rules."

Mr. Paulsen began putting away the tools we'd used. "I'm sure there is a way, but Mrs. Paulsen and I made our deal with the devil when we moved into this neighborhood, and we're obliged to keep it, I'm afraid."

Walking upstairs, I felt better than I had in days. It had felt good to hammer in a few nails, build a thing that could be of use. Mr. Paulsen had said that's what he'd liked best about raising chickens when he was a kid, that it had made him feel useful every time he held an egg in his hand before he took it up to the house to give to his mother.

I stored the box under my bed. I didn't have anything to put in it, but I pulled it out to look about twenty times that weekend. There's something satisfying about a box you've made yourself.

Monday at school Henry gave me a plastic bag with one of Miss Blue's green eggs in it. Henry and Harrison were taking care of my chickens for me while I was staying at the Paulsens'. I knew Henry'd been over at Granny's that weekend, or else how'd he get the egg, but

I didn't ask him any questions. I didn't want to hear word one about Granny.

Henry showed me the pinpricks on each end of the egg, one small, one big, where he'd blown out the yolk and the white.

"An empty egg, my man," he'd said, handing the bag to me. "That's got to be a symbol for something."

That afternoon I put Miss Blue's egg in the box. I put the box on my bed, and I stared at it for a long time. While I was sitting there, Mrs. Paulsen knocked on the door and peeked in. "I've just made peanut-butter cookies," she said. "Would you like some?"

I nodded. Mrs. Paulsen brought in a plate of cookies and a glass of milk and set them down on the bedside table. Then she looked inside the box.

"What a beautiful egg," she said. "Is it from an Araucana?"

"Her name is Miss Blue," I said. "She's real smart for a chicken."

"I always thought chickens were smart," Mrs. Paulsen said. "It's simply a different kind of smart from, say, a dog or a cat. It takes them longer to figure things out. But they always do."

I didn't have anything else to put in my box until the next week, when we had our first night of family counseling. A judge had ordered us to go twice a week, and we had to keep it up for three months. If we did good, then the therapist would write a report back to the judge. A good report meant I got to go home.

Mr. Paulsen drove. That first night he brought a copy of *National Geographic,* a copy of *Newsweek,* and coffee in a travel mug. He said, "Good luck, Tobin," when I got out of the car, and gave me one of them bows of his. I bowed back and went inside.

Daddy was waiting for me in the lobby. He handed me a pack of NASCAR trading cards. "They'll be worth a lot of money someday, that's what I keep hearing." I rubbed my thumb over the cellophane wrapper. I thought maybe I'd put the cards in the box when I got home. Wouldn't even open the pack, to keep it fresh.

The family therapist's name was Ms. Hill. She reminded me a little bit of Miss Thesman, the way she was corny and sincere. You could tell she wanted to be our family's hero. "I'm here to help you," she said very first thing. "I'm here to keep you together, not tear you apart."

Nobody looked like they much believed her. That first session, we spent most of our time staring at Ms. Hill, shifting around in our uncomfortable chairs, waiting for her to fix us. Ms. Hill stared back, like she was daring us to say something.

After about ten minutes of our little staring game, Daddy looked at his watch and stood up. "This is a waste of my time."

Ms. Hill gave Daddy a hard look. "Is your family a waste of your time?"

Daddy sat back down.

Then Ms. Hill started asking us questions about ourselves and about one another. She asked me what my first memory of Patrick was, and she asked Daddy what were the things Summer cared about most when she was ten years old. It was like a quiz show, except we were the only people in the world who knew the answers.

When I went back out to the car that night,

Mr. Paulsen was just finishing up his *National Geographic*. He handed it to me as I got in. "There's an interesting article about modern-day pirates in here. Did you know there was such a thing?"

I flipped through a few pages, checking out the pictures. "I didn't even know till a couple of years ago that there were real pirates. I always thought pirates were make-believe."

Mr. Paulsen tapped the magazine with his finger. "You can learn a lot by reading *National Geographic*," he said. Then he started the engine. I half expected him to take me to my real house, my head was so caught up in all the questions Ms. Hill had been asking, but we went back to the shiny suburbs, where Mrs. Paulsen was waiting for me with a piece of coconut-cream pie.

It got to be a habit for me and Mr. Paulsen to discuss the articles in *National Geographic* as we drove to and from family therapy. We talked about people hiding out in caves and monks who lived on mountain tops and sea creatures so ugly even their own mothers probably didn't love them. It was relaxing for me to discuss topics that were a million miles away from my real life.

At our third session, Ms. Hill sat down, crossed her legs, and said, "Tell me some stories about Sandy."

Daddy went pale. I felt my throat freeze up. But Shane leaned forward and said in a low, steady voice, "My mama loved to barbecue."

It was like he'd been waiting a long, long time to say that.

"Tell me more, Shane," Ms. Hill said, like a detective who'd stumbled onto some big clue in the case she was trying to solve.

"My mama would call people every weekend to come cook out," Shane said. "She even cooked out on Thanksgiving. She had one of them big turkey grills, an outdoor roaster? She loved that thing, man."

"She used it all year round," Summer put in. "Thanksgiving, Christmas, Easter, even the Fourth of July one year. I got tired of all that turkey, if you want to know the truth."

Ms. Hill looked at me like it was my turn. I pulled at an invisible thread on my T-shirt and cleared my throat a couple times. It hadn't been a problem to tell Henry and Harrison stories about my mom when I was writing an auto-biography, but there was something about having to talk about her in front of my family that made my stomach feel tight. My mom was a topic we'd all been avoiding for a long time.

"What I remember about Mama's cookouts is that when the weather was good, there'd always be five or six families there, and all the kids would play football or hotbox or whatever game it was the season for," I said when I finally got some words to come out of my mouth. "Just about any Saturday night when it wasn't raining or snowing, my mom would haul the grill out to the middle of the backyard and send us kids around to the neighbors to see if they wanted to join in. Hardly nobody would when it was cold, but if you had a warm night in May or June, you can bet we had every family on our road out there."

My favorite part was after we were done eating. The grown-ups would pull their lawn chairs into a circle and talk about work and their kids and the crazy stuff that'd happened over the years. The ones who drank beer would get louder and louder as it got darker, their wives hushing them, but laughing, too.

All the kids would be juiced up on hot dogs and Cokes and marshmallows roasted over the grill. We'd play one game after the other—freeze tag, swing the statue, dodgeball—getting wilder and wilder, the littlest ones shrieking like monkeys from excitement. "Somebody's gonna get hurt," the grown-ups would call out, but nobody ever did.

My mom was the center of it all, cooking hamburgers, spooning out baked beans, telling funny stories about the customers at the Food Lion, where she was a cashier. People were always asking her to remember stuff that happened. "Hey, Sandy," somebody would say, "tell about the time the power went out and Rich Humphreys dumped ten pounds of rib roast in the creek to keep it cold." My mom could take a story you'd told her and make it a hundred times better.

"You remember how we'd all clean up afterwards, and Mama would be sitting in a lawn chair and she'd always say, 'You all don't have to do that, we can get it in the morning'?" Shane asked.

"And Daddy would always say how in the morning we'd all be too fat to do much of anything," Patrick added.

I looked over at Daddy, waiting for him to add in his part of the story. I wanted the talk about my mom to keep going. Daddy was looking out the window, his eyes not focused on anything in particular. I was thinking he might say something about how every once in a while, if somebody was playing music on a boom box and a slow song came on, he'd grab Mama by the waist and pull her close, waltzing her across the grass. That was a good memory, and one I wouldn't have minded to hear him talk about.

But he didn't say a word. Just sat there quiet as two A.M., like maybe he'd forgotten everything good that had happened to us.

I didn't figure there was any way I'd be going home in three months, not if my daddy was as empty as a blown-out eggshell and couldn't ever be filled up again.

TWENTY-THREE

When Harrison finally sold him some eggs, it was like somebody set him on fire, son. He started planning a chicken empire bigger than Nebraska.

"Here's a memo for you," Henry said in English class, handing me the third memo Harrison had sent me that week. "Has to do with employee cleanliness. It's next to employee godliness, dude."

I read half a paragraph about the importance of hand washing before and after handling eggs, then shoved the memo into my notebook. The last one had been about upgrading our business communications. Harrison was of the opinion I needed me an e-mail account so he could send me hourly updates on how selling a dozen eggs a week to his cake-baking neighbor Mrs. Trellis was going to make us millionaires before you knew it.

Henry leaned across the aisle and tapped his pen on my arm. "Harrison wants to know if you'll ask those people you're staying with to get on our egg list. A dozen farm-fresh eggs a week for four bucks, it's a hard-to-beat offer."

"I don't know," I said. "They might do it just to be nice even if they don't need the eggs. I don't want to put any pressure on 'em. Besides, it's not like the Paulsens live next door, like the lady who's buying eggs from Harrison. How'd we even get the eggs to them fresh?"

"We'd figure something out. But how about this—I'll tell Harrison he has to come over and make the sales pitch himself. You don't have to worry about guilt-tripping anybody into buying anything, and Harrison can practice wheeling and dealing."

The next afternoon Mrs. Otis dropped Henry and Harrison off at the Paulsens'. They'd never been to my real house. Here it was, first time they'd come to where I lived, and where I lived was at a stranger's house.

As soon as he was in the front door, Harrison gave Mrs. Paulsen a brochure he'd made in the computer lab at school. It had charts and graphs and a list of why buying fresh, organic chicken eggs was the best thing you could do for your health and spiritual well-being. I grabbed a plate of banana bread and led Henry to the wide-screen TV.

Henry sprawled out on the couch, like he was planning on staying for a while, maybe forever. "My man, this is the life. I mean, I've seen cars smaller than that TV screen." He grabbed a piece of banana bread off the plate, shoved half of it into his mouth, and looked around the room. "Do you think about what it would be like to live here full time?" he asked after he'd swallowed. "I mean, what happens if the judge gives your dad the thumbs-down?"

"I don't know what happens," I told Henry, sinking into an easy chair. "I don't know if they'd keep me here or not."

I had to admit, I'd wondered what it would

be like to live at the Paulsens' for real, food coming at me left and right, building stuff with Mr. Paulsen in the garage, Mrs. Paulsen peeking into my room at night after she thought I'd gone to sleep. But then I'd remember about my dad filling up the kitchen cabinets with maple-flavored baked beans and Hamburger Helper, trying to make our house okay for a family to live in, and I felt bad for even thinking about living anywhere else.

That night when Mr. Paulsen drove me to family therapy, I studied his face when he wasn't looking. I didn't have one doubt that he'd been a good dad to his sons. If I'd been his son, he'd have been a good dad to me too. But I wasn't his. The people I belonged to were waiting over in Ms. Hill's office, squirming in them uncomfortable chairs, trying to figure out how to make our family work.

"Are we gonna talk about Mama some more tonight?" Patrick asked as soon as Ms. Hill sat down with her notepad and pencil at the ready. "Because there's some people who say the past ought to be left past."

"Is that what you think, Patrick?" Ms. Hill asked.

Patrick nodded. "Yeah, pretty much. But if we're gonna go on and on about it, I got something I've been meaning to tell you all."

"Spill it, little brother," Shane said from across the room. "It can't be too bad."

"Ain't bad for me," Patrick said. "It's bad for you. Because what you all probably don't know is, I was always Mama's favorite." He crossed his arms, like he was daring somebody to say otherwise.

"What makes you think you were Mama's favorite?" I asked him. Made me a little mad he could believe such a thing was true. "Mama didn't have no favorites."

"Oh, yes she did," Patrick said, sounding firm about it. "And it just happened to be me. And how I know it is that she used to come kidnap me from school."

Shane laughed. "You're making that up, Pat. No way Mama ever came and took you out of school. The only way she'd ever let anybody miss school was if that person was throwing up.

She respected throwing up. Otherwise, man, you were out the door and on the bus, no matter how bad you felt."

Patrick got a stubborn look on his face. "She kidnapped me out of school all right. Her and Granny did once and took me to the state fair. I was in third grade, in Mrs. Holland's class. Girl came down from the principal's office with a note saying there was some sort of family problem. Wasn't no problem, it was just Granny and Mama. Both of 'em called in sick to work so they could go to the fair. Decided to take me with 'em. I got a picture hidden away of me and Mama riding the elephant."

He turned to me. "You know how they have elephant rides at the fair, right?"

I nodded, and Patrick nodded, too, like I'd just backed up his whole story.

"But what I remember most about that whole trip is that on the way home we got a flat tire. Mama and Granny was both out there on the side of the highway, trying to work that jack, just laughing and cussing a blue streak. I didn't even know Mama knew words like that."

I heard a snort from the corner and turned to see Daddy covering a smile with his hand. Patrick heard it, too. "Did you know she could cuss like that, Daddy?" he asked. Daddy just nodded.

"The other thing, how I knew I was Mama's favorite?" Patrick went on, turning back to the rest of us. "Is she used to let me stay up till midnight on account that midnight was always my natural bedtime, even when I was a baby."

That made Daddy laugh some more. He leaned forward in his chair. "I remember when you were still little you'd fall asleep around eight o'clock on the couch with your head in Sandy's lap, and she wouldn't let anybody move you for the world. After the news, she'd carry you back to your room."

Daddy ran his hand through his hair, like he was trying to pull thoughts from his head. "I don't know what happened," his voice all serious now. "One day she was healthy, holding you kids on her lap, and the next day she was lying in a hospital bed. Only thing I know for sure is that I should've taken better care

189

of her, made her go to the doctor sooner."

He looked out the window. Headlights flashed across his face, but it was like he didn't see them. "We didn't have any money when she started feeling so bad. I'd just started working again after being laid off for nearly half a year. But I should've done something."

We all sat there, mouths shut tight. Then Shane started shaking his head, frowning hard.

"You ain't remembering right," he said to Daddy. "You ain't remembering it right at all." Daddy's eyes opened wide, like he'd just come out of a hard sleep. "She'd been feeling sick a long time before she even told anybody about it. I knew something was wrong with her. I was in seventh grade, taking that North Carolina history class, and she used to help me with it all the time. She'd come home from work and drill me about every single North Carolina fact that ever was."

Shane turned and looked at me. "You taking that class now?" I nodded. "Well, if Mama was here, you'd be getting an A. She was like the queen of North Carolina or something. And then

190

all the sudden she stopped helping me. She'd come home and go to sleep. Daddy was working some second-shift job, and me and Summer would have to fix dinner."

Summer laughed at that. "You didn't ever once fix dinner, Shane. You just poured the tea into the glasses. I remember that napping, though, since you brought it up. That went on for a long time. I remember saying something to Granny about it, and she said maybe Mama was pregnant."

"That's what I thought, too," Daddy said. He rubbed his eyes. "I forgot about that part. She was sleeping a lot on the weekends, and I thought, 'Please don't let it be another baby.'"

Shane nodded, like he thought Daddy was finally seeing the light. "And then when she did finally say something about feeling sick, you called up Granny because Mama wouldn't listen to you about going to see a doctor. Granny took her to the doctor the next day."

"Man, how you remember all this stuff?" Patrick asked. "It's like you got some superhero memory power."

Shane chewed on a fingernail. "I remember everything about it," he said. "From the first to the last."

That night I went home and took my autobiography out of my backpack, where I'd been keeping it ever since Miss Thesman handed it back to me. On the back of the last page I started writing down our barbecue story. Needed two more pages to finish it. Then I got out a fresh sheet and wrote down about when my mom got sick.

And then I put my autobiography in the box.

At the next session, Ms. Hill gave our family an assignment. She said we had to make a date to go through Mama's closet and get rid of most of the stuff.

"It's been five years, Randy," she said, staring Daddy down. "It's time."

Daddy looked at his shoes, like they'd gotten real interesting all the sudden. But that Saturday during my visiting time we did it—me, Daddy, Shane, and Summer. Patrick stood in the doorway and watched. We took out the clothes and put them in boxes, all but a few things Summer

192

wanted to keep, a peach-colored slip and two sweaters.

"You gonna give one of them boxes to Granny?" I asked Daddy after we'd gotten everything packed away. "For that quilt she wants to do?"

Daddy gave me a steady look. "There ain't no quilt, son. Never was a quilt, never would be one, even if I gave your granny an attic full of clothes."

"So why does she want the clothes, then?"

"She don't want the clothes," Daddy said, lifting one of the boxes onto his shoulder. "She wants Sandy. That's two different things completely."

TWENTY-FOUR

You might not know it, but you can get to missing a chicken.

I didn't have one intention of going to Granny's house again, but I kept wondering how Miss Blue and the rest of them was doing. Not to mention I had to work up an oral report for Mr. Peabody, and how was I supposed to do that without having my chickens to study on?

First time I went, Mrs. Paulsen drove me after school. She waited in the car with a book while I went out back. I was hoping Granny wouldn't be there, but I saw her through the kitchen window. She waved. I didn't bother waving back.

"You gonna stand in my backyard and ignore me to my face?" she called a few minutes later from the porch.

I looked up at her, shading my eyes from the sun. She wanted to talk, fine. "Is it true you wanted custody of me just to get back at Daddy for not giving you Mama's clothes?"

Granny's eyes got all squinty, like she was confused about something. "No, that wasn't it at all," she told me. "Is that what your no-good daddy said?"

And I said, "Stop calling him no-good. He's pretty good. He's getting better."

Granny turned and went inside. End of conversation.

This last time I went to visit my chickens, I didn't expect to exchange a single word with Granny. But I'd only been there a few minutes when I could feel Granny watching me from the porch. When she finally went in the house, I figured that was that, but she came back, this time carrying something in her hand. "Come on up here for a minute, son," she called to me. "I've got something I want to give you."

I trudged up the hill to the house, thinking there wasn't one thing she had to give me that I had the least bit of interest in taking.

I stood on the bottom step and put my hand out. Granny leaned down and handed me a picture. It was my parents on their wedding day. My dad's face wasn't cut out. It was right there, next to my mom's. They both looked young and happy, their arms around each other, big smiles stretched across their faces.

"Mama sure was pretty," I said, holding the picture close to my face, like maybe I could step inside it if I tried hard enough.

Granny sat down on the step and stared off into the trees. "That girl right there, she was my only child. She was my baby. I have lost two husbands, one by death, the other by divorce, and I have lost my parents and my brothers and sisters. But nothing ever pierced me to the core like that little girl's dying. I know it wasn't your daddy's fault. I know I messed up by filing a report with Social Services. Is that what you want to hear? Is that what it takes for you not to be mad at me?"

I didn't say anything. Didn't want to give her the pleasure of me forgiving her. I held on to that feeling for as long as I could, and then I looked at that picture of my parents. Thought about how it would be a nice thing to put in my box. That's when something hard inside of me broke open. Leaning down, I brushed some dirt off my shoe. "I might be mad at you for a while longer, I ain't sure," I said.

Granny nodded, like she understood. Then she swiped her hand across her eyes. She pointed to Calvin. "I believe that dog has got egg envy. I caught him sitting on a nest yesterday, practically squawking with the effort of laying."

I sat down next to her on the step. She put out her hand. I put my hand in it. We sat that way for a while, and then I said I needed to see my chickens.

I had to give my report in the morning. Henry'd already given his. I could still picture it, him walking to the front of the room, applause popping out here and there, and a few boos, too. Henry took a deep bow. "My friends and fellow scientists, today I will present to you the soul of a chicken." He pulled out a stack of charts from behind Mr. Peabody's desk. "But first let us begin with the chicken brain, a compact marvel of sense and sensibility."

I leaned back in my chair. I could hear people shuffling in their seats up and down the aisles. A pencil dropped, and then another. I wondered if Henry had given a lot of thought to his audience, a bunch of seventh graders hopped up on chewing gum and Reese's Pieces. Maybe not the biggest convention of chicken lovers in the world. But then Henry wouldn't care if they loved chickens or not. He just wanted them to understand chickens.

My chickens started to cluck and fuss as I walked down the yard. I wondered what they'd think if they knew tomorrow they were going to be the subject of a big, scientific presentation.

Only maybe they wouldn't be. I didn't know how much scientific stuff I had to say about them. Mostly what I'd learned by having chickens is that you could love some things you'd never guess. You might not think you could love a chicken. A dog, sure. Everybody loves dogs. But a chicken? For a long time I didn't even think a chicken had a soul. Brain the size of a pea. A heart that thumped for nobody but itself.

Miss Blue began to peck hard at the ground. A worm stretched out of the dirt, caught in her beak, and that made the other chickens gather around her, just one big gaggle of cheerleaders. Calvin barked. I got all wrapped up in it too, like I was watching an Olympic competition and Miss Blue was going for the gold.

All my life I'd been around my granny's chickens, or at least could see them way out there in the very back of her yard, but they hadn't interested me. Maybe it was because I'd never sat down in the dirt with them and watched them go about their business or tried to make some conversation. Or maybe it was because I'd seen Granny kill a chicken by twisting off its head with her bare hands. It was like she was wringing out a dish towel. How could I get interested in chickens when I'd seen a sight like that?

"You can't expect a person to love an animal they might see decapitated at any minute. It ain't realistic," I told Miss Blue, who was gulping down her worm. She looked up at me like it shocked her to learn that some chickens got treated that way.

I stepped onto an old tree stump. "Here is a scientific fact," I told the chickens, pretending they were my classmates. "I used to not like chickens, and now I do."

Calvin barked again, and I wondered if he'd been the very same way. I continued. "I used to think chickens were dumb, and now I don't. I never would have thought you could be friends with a chicken, but now I do think that. So how come I changed my mind?"

A horn honked up in the driveway. When I turned around, there was Harrison sitting in the driver's seat of Granny's truck. "Hey, Tobin," he called out. "You want a ride?"

"I'm giving a speech," I yelled back, and that about cracked me up. I was giving a speech to a bunch of chickens. On top of that, I was pretty sure they could understand every word I was saying. I'd use that as proof in my report. If chickens could listen, didn't that mean they could think?

I turned back to the chickens. Lefty was looking at me with her head cocked. It appeared she couldn't wait to hear what I had to say next. "Maybe I changed my mind about chickens because taking care of chickens got me off my butt," I announced, and something about Lefty's expression made me think she appreciated that answer. But I wasn't sure if it was the right one. Maybe I got to liking chickens because my chickens were like me. Not as dumb or prehistoric as you might think after you studied on them some.

You'd be surprised how many people don't know the first thing about chickens.

"Tobin, my man!"

I turned around to see Henry walking down the hill. I could tell by the look on his face he had some big idea he wanted to tell me about. But the second he opened his mouth, Granny's truck muttered and grumbled, and there was old Harrison smiling at us through the windshield, waving like he was about to take off into the wild blue yonder.

Me and Henry started running. I heard Granny yell, "What the Sam Hill . . . ?" and then

she was hauling tail out the back do
chickens were clucking and racing us
hill, and Calvin was barking his head off.
took Granny a second to reach the tru
grab the keys out of the ignition. It about
me and Henry up, the look on Harrison's
guessed Granny must have turned a new
she wasn't going to let Harrison learn to

Henry threw himself down on the g
"Tobin, my man," he huffed, his chest v
ing in and out like an accordion, "for ou
project, I think we ought to teach our ch
to sing. Not like people, but like singing b
read something about how you can do th

I sat down next to him. "Easier than
ing them how to read," I said.

"Hey, that's not a bad idea either."
grinned, like he was picturing Miss Blue ho
open a copy of *Romeo and Juliet*. "If anybody
teach a chicken to read, it would be me and

Hard to argue with that, son.

I turned back to the chickens. Lefty was looking at me with her head cocked. It appeared she couldn't wait to hear what I had to say next. "Maybe I changed my mind about chickens because taking care of chickens got me off my butt," I announced, and something about Lefty's expression made me think she appreciated that answer. But I wasn't sure if it was the right one. Maybe I got to liking chickens because my chickens were like me. Not as dumb or prehistoric as you might think after you studied on them some.

You'd be surprised how many people don't know the first thing about chickens.

"Tobin, my man!"

I turned around to see Henry walking down the hill. I could tell by the look on his face he had some big idea he wanted to tell me about. But the second he opened his mouth, Granny's truck muttered and grumbled, and there was old Harrison smiling at us through the windshield, waving like he was about to take off into the wild blue yonder.

Me and Henry started running. I heard Granny yell, "What the Sam Hill . . . ?" and then she was hauling tail out the back door. The chickens were clucking and racing us up the hill, and Calvin was barking his head off. It only took Granny a second to reach the truck and grab the keys out of the ignition. It about busted me and Henry up, the look on Harrison's face. I guessed Granny must have turned a new leaf if she wasn't going to let Harrison learn to drive.

Henry threw himself down on the ground. "Tobin, my man," he huffed, his chest wheezing in and out like an accordion, "for our next project, I think we ought to teach our chickens to sing. Not like people, but like singing birds. I read something about how you can do that."

I sat down next to him. "Easier than teaching them how to read," I said.

"Hey, that's not a bad idea either." Henry grinned, like he was picturing Miss Blue holding open a copy of *Romeo and Juliet*. "If anybody could teach a chicken to read, it would be me and you."

Hard to argue with that, son.

DAYS